WOMEN WHO RUN WITH THE WEREWOLVES

Women who run with the Werewolves

Tales of Blood, Lust and Metamorphosis

edited by
Pam Keesey

CLEIS
[PRESS]

Published in the United States by Cleis Press Inc., P.O. Box 8933, Pittsburgh, Pennsylvania 15221, and P.O. Box 14684, San Francisco, California 94114.
Printed in the United States.
Cover and text design: Frank Wiedemann
Logo art: Juana Alicia
First Edition.
10 9 8 7 6 5 4 3 2 1

"The Wife's Story" by Ursula K. Le Guin is reprinted by permission of the author.

"Boobs" by Suzy McKee Charnas was first published in *Asimov's Science Fiction*, July 1989, and is reprinted by permission of the author.

Excerpt from *Wilding* by Melanie Tem. Copyright 1992 by Melanie Tem. Used by permission of Dell Books, a division of Bantam Doubleday Dell Publishing Group, Inc.

Thanks to Natalie Op de Beeck for a great title; my parents, Janne, and my friends and colleagues at the Resource Center of The Americas for their unparalleled support; Tracy Peterson for typing above and beyond the call of duty, and for answering all of my medical questions; Mike Callies, my personal pop-culture guru; and Peter Larsen of Dreamhaven Books.

Library of Congress Cataloging-in-Publication Data

Women who run with the werewolves : tales of blood, lust, and metamorphosis / edited by Pam Keesey. — 1st ed.
    p.   cm.
  ISBN 1-57344-057-4 (paper).
  1. Werewolves—Fiction. 2. Horror tales, American.
3. Metamorphosis—Fiction. 4. Women—Fiction. I. Keesey, Pam, 1964-
PS648.W37W66   1996
813' .0873808375—dc20   96-27116
                                                            CIP

Contents

Dedicated to Forrest J Ackerman—
an inspiration and a favorite uncle to generations
of monster-loving kids like me.
Happy 80th Birthday, Dear Forry!

Introduction

I am like the she-wolf.
I broke with the pack
And fled to the mountains
Tired of the plain....

Poor little tame sheep in a flock!
Don't fear the she-wolf, she will not harm you.
But also don't belittle her, her teeth are sharp
And in the forest she learned to be sly.

Alfonsina Storni, 1882-1938
Argentinian poet

Even the most repressed woman has a secret life, with secret thoughts and secret feelings which are lush and wild, that is, natural. Even the most captured woman guards the place of the wildish self, for she knows intuitively that someday there will be a loophole, an aperture, a chance, and she will hightail it to escape.

Clarissa Pinkola Estés
Women Who Run with the Wolves

I, like so many others, am a child of *Famous Monsters of Filmland.* First published in 1958, *Famous Monsters* magazine featured the great monster movies of the thirties, forties and fifties. At the top of the heap were the classic horror films of Universal Studios—*Dracula* starring Bela Lugosi; *Frankenstein* and *Bride of Frankenstein* starring Boris Karloff; and *The Wolfman* starring Lon Chaney Jr. Thanks to *Famous Monsters* and its esteemed editor, Forrest J Ackerman, affectionately known as Forry by millions of fans, kids like me grew up surrounded by monster-movie classics. Although my first love is and always will be the vampire, my diversion into werewolf lore is really no diversion at all, but another opportunity to indulge myself in my lifelong love of all monsters great and small.

After deciding to edit this collection of stories, I sought out Clarissa Pinkola Estés' *Women Who Run with the Wolves*. The power of Estés' message and its resounding impact are attested to by the success of her book. *Women Who Run with the Wolves* has sold millions of copies, spent two years on the *New York Times* bestseller list, and has been translated into some twenty-seven languages. Estés' primary message is that the Wild Woman—"the wild, natural, powerful force within each woman filled with good instincts, passionate creativity, and ageless knowing"—is an endangered species. Throughout the book, Estés stresses the importance of reclaiming the Wild Woman, for without her, women become "over-domesticated, fearful, uncreative, trapped."

The title for Estés' book came from her study of wildlife biology. In wolves, Estés sees a metaphor for the history of women:

> Healthy wolves and healthy women share certain psychic characteristics: keen sensing, playful spirit, and a heightened capacity for devotion. Wolves and women are relational by nature, inquiring, possessed of great endurance and strength…. They are experienced in adapting to constantly changing circumstances: they are fiercely stalwart and very brave.
>
> Yet both have been hounded, harassed, and falsely imputed to be devouring and devious, overly aggressive, of less value than those who are their detractors.

Even in the most wounded woman and the most damaged of psyches, the Wild Woman exists. She can never be completely destroyed. She may go into hiding, but she continues to live on. The Wild Woman, like a rabid or injured wolf, compensates for the loss of her natural, healthy state:

> There is no way to fool the Wild Woman…. She is aware of the dark bundles in a woman's mind that are tied round and round with ropes and bands. These spaces in a woman's mind do not respond to light or grace, so covered over are they. And,

of course, since the psyche is greatly compensatory, the secret will find its way out anyway, if not in actual words, then in the form of sudden melancholias, intermittent and mysterious rages, all sorts of physical tics, torques, and pains....

The central message of Estés' book is that each one of us needs to retrieve the Wild Woman, to rediscover our wolfish selves. We, as women, have been cut off from our instinctual selves, and to retrieve and to nurture the Wild Woman, we must enter our own darkness; we must be prepared to encounter our rabid, distorted selves, to come face to face with our powerful, rage-filled selves. "A woman must go into the dark," she writes, "but at the same time she must not be irreparably trapped, captured, or killed on her way there or back."

The "beast within" is a classic theme in werewolf literature and folklore. The notion that we have a dual nature is a common one, and beast images exist throughout the world in all cultures. The Northern and Eastern European image is the wolf; while in Central America, it may be a jaguar or a puma; the bear in Russia; and the hyena in Africa. The supernatural lore of humans turning into animals and animals into humans is a universal archetype. These totemic beliefs date back to ancient history, when the power of the animal spirit may have been called upon for its skills and attributes. A wolf, for example, could be called upon for its hunting skills, cunning and strength. Over the millennia, this image of the human animal has metamorphosed and transmuted into what has become common fare for horror novels and monster films.

Lycanthropy—the medical condition associated with being a werewolf—is very similar to what Estés is describing. The origins of the word *lycanthropy* come from the Greek *lukanthropia—lykos* meaning wolf, and *anthropos* meaning human. The name for both a psychiatric condition and a supernatural one, lycanthropia is one of the oldest diagnoses in what is thought of as psychiatric literature, with records of individuals being diagnosed as lycanthropic as early as the fifth century AD. Early diagnoses of lycanthropy described any kind of animalistic behavior on the part of the patient, with symptoms including fits, delusions and aggressive behavior.

In his book, *The Beast Within: A History of the Werewolf,* Adam Douglas describes the case of a forty-nine-year-old woman who was convinced she was turning into a wolf:

During the twenty years of her marriage, she had been troubled by urges toward bestiality, lesbianism, and adultery, as well as by an obsession with wolves which led her to think and dream about them constantly. Eventually she acted on her impulses, tearing off her clothes at a family gathering, and adopting the mating position of a female wolf in front of her mother. The next day, after sexual intercourse with her husband, she spent two hours growling, scratching and gnawing at the bed.... Her delusions persisted for a few weeks and she was able to describe them in some detail: "I am a world of the night: I am a wolf woman of the day...I have claws, teeth, fangs, hair...and anguish is my prey at night...the gnashing and snarling of teeth...powerless is my cause. I am what I am and will always roam the earth long after death...I will continue to search for perfection and salvation...."

This woman, who had for years repressed inner compulsions and desires, found herself in a psychic and spiritual state in which she literally believed herself to be out at night, running with wolves.

Estés describes the Wild Woman as having "real teeth, a true snarl, huge generosity, unequaled hearing, sharp claws, generous and furry breasts." This image of the Wild Woman as both nurturing mother and feral beast has its roots, like the vampire, in the traditions of the ancient goddesses. In myth and folklore, dogs and wolves, both carrion eaters, were believed to carry the dead in their bodies to their mother, the Goddess. Sometimes, she was a dog herself—a bitch-goddess such as the Vedic Sarama. As the Huntress—Artemis, Diana, or Anath—the Goddess is also accompanied by dogs. In Celtic tradition, the Goddess Hel, ruler of the land of death, gave birth to lunar wolf-dogs who ate the flesh of the dead and carried souls to paradise. These dogs came to be known as the Hounds of Hel, and later, the Hounds of Hell. They accompanied the Goddess and assisted her in guarding the gates of the afterworld.

In wolf-guise, these goddesses are all variations on the Dark Goddess, the Devouring Mother. She is death personified, and to enter the realm of her darkness is to enter death itself.

Early images of the Goddess also included the wolf-god as her male consort. Males who were dedicated to the worship of the Goddess in her wolf form are often associated with early man-wolf imagery. As Christianity made inroads into pagan and Goddess-worshipping cultures, wolves and their man-wolf images became associated with the Devil. In the years between 1520 and 1630, an estimated thirty thousand cases of werewolves were recorded in France alone. Werewolves, the Devil's creatures, were believed to aid and abet witches in their "evil deeds." Many women were accused of "riding a wolf," the implication being that they were on their way to a witches' sabbat. Although some women were accused of being werewolves, the majority of women condemned during this time were accused of being witches. Mostly men were accused of being werewolves. The persistence of the archetypal image of the Goddess and her wolf consort may explain, at least in part, why werewolves are, more often than not, men.

The classic female werewolf has a lot in common with the classic *femme fatale.* One of the earliest werewolf stories to appear in English is an often-reprinted excerpt from the novel *The Phantom Ship* (1839) by Captain Frederick Marryat. A young man, Krantz, tells the tale of his father's marriage to a Nordic woman named Christina. The father's first wife died in mysterious circumstances, and he has sworn not to harm Christina in any way. One day, in their father's absence, Christina kills Krantz's brother and sister and eats their remains. When Krantz's father realizes what has happened, he kills Christina, only to be killed later by the avenging spirits of the North who had accepted his oath to bring no harm to her. Thus, Christina—beautiful though cruel and cold, much like the *femme fatale* of romantic literature—became the model for female werewolves in the stories that followed.

Many nineteenth-century werewolf tales featured women who were the exact opposite of the Victorian convention of frail womanhood. In "The Man-Wolf" (1864), written by the French writing team of Erckmann-Chatrian, a nobleman's lust for a female werewolf leads him to murder his wife, marry the werewolf, and father a generation of wolf-children. "Olalla" (1885) by Robert Louis Stevenson is the story of a family presumed affected by madness and degeneracy. Both stories portray women who are driven by something deep within their psyches to strike out at the world. In Clemence Housman's play, *The Were-wolf* (1895), a young woman who wears white furs and is known as White Fell appears in a Nordic village. She is described as "a powerful, independent woman, a prototype of the barbaric heroines of many epics to follow, a fur-slinging, axe-wielding huntress descended straight from Hyperborea."

Female werewolves made frequent appearances in the pulp fiction magazines of the early 1900s. Writers such as Greye La Spina, Seabury Quinn, H. Warner Munn and Jack Williamson contributed to werewolf lore and magazines such as *Weird Tales, Strange Tales, Famous Fantastic Mysteries* and others that appeared in the years between the mid-1920s and the late 1950s. Princess Tchernova, the principal character in La Spina's *Invaders from the Dark*, is a classic *femme fatale*. She has sharp, white teeth, green eyes, red lips, and highly polished fingernails. La Spina writes "even the princess' slinking, sinuous walk...by its resemblance to the tireless gait of the wolf, would have betrayed her real personality to an expert."

In the latter part of the twentieth century, the werewolf will be forever associated with the Universal Studios' movie, *The Wolfman* in which Lon Chaney Jr. portrayed the sympathetic werewolf, a victim of circumstance. "Whomever is bitten by a werewolf and lives, becomes a werewolf himself," Maleva (the old gypsy woman, played by Maria Ouspenskaya) tells Lon Chaney's Larry Talbot. The film ends with the elder Talbot, Larry's father, bludgeoning a wolf with a silver-tipped cane. Talbot's father then watches in horror as the wolfman's body transforms in death to that of his son, Larry. With the success of *The Wolfman,* Larry Talbot became the prototype for the werewolf as tragic hero, a sympathetic beast who is also a victim.

As with so many successful films, *The Wolfman* was followed by a number of imitators. Among them were films that featured women as werewolves. In *She-Wolf of London* (1946) and *Daughter of Dr. Jekyll* (1957), young women fear that they have inherited a family curse of the werewolf. As grisly murders take place, they are sure that they are responsible. Both, however, are redeemed in the end. Ostensibly a vampire movie, *Blood of Dracula* (1957) has much more in common with the werewolf motif: When a young woman is recruited for an experiment that brings about physical and psychological changes, she becomes hairy, with a heavy brow and ferocious teeth and an insatiable need for human blood. Her only salvation is her ultimate death.

Other werewolf movies portray women in more licentious ways. The transformation of women into beasts correlates with their sexual arousal in films such as *Cry of the Werewolf* (1944) and *El Festin de la Loba* (1964). In *The Howling* (1980), Elisabeth Brooks portrays a werewolf who is also a classic vamp, the sexually insatiable woman who ruins and destroys men in the midst of her frenzied bloodlust. This equation of women's sexual urges with bestiality is not limited to werewolves—in films such as *Cat People, Attack of the Cobra Woman* and *Lair of the White Worm,* women's sexuality is characterized in terms of animal behavior, with cats and snakes seeming to provide the most popular comparisons.

Not always a tragedy, the transformation into a werewolf often represents freedom and a return to nature. In *Wolf,* Laura Alden (Michelle Pfeiffer) is completely unhappy with her life, her relationship with her father, and is still grieving the death of her brother. She meets and falls in love with Will Randall (Jack Nicholson) who is, by that time, well into his transformation into a wolf. By the end of the film, it is clear that she is not at all afraid of the likelihood that she, too, may be a werewolf, but is instead drawn to the freedom that the transformation represents.

The idea that animal transformation is freeing appears from time to time in werewolf literature and is most often used as a symbol of ostracism, the means by which an individual is kept apart from society. For Estés, freedom is the essence of transformation. The Wild Woman as creature, or *criatura,* lives a life with innate integrity and natural boundaries. Despite the risk of confronting the *criatura*— who is the death goddess, the maiden in descent, the crone—we all benefit from listening to her wisdom.

The stories in this collection represent a wide range of beliefs about werewolves. As change and transformation are central themes to the werewolf mythos so is the change that we all go through as young adults—puberty—a recurring theme in much of werewolf literature. "Boobs" by Suzy McKee Charnas conveys the heart-wrenching experience of Kelsey, a junior-high-school girl whose body is changing from the pre-pubescent, athletic body that she knew and loved to a body that is bringing unwanted attention from boys. In "Breaking the Circle," Michael Lucas writes of Chris, a young woman who must confront indifference, anger and abuse stemming from her parent's inability to accept her for who—and what—she really is. In Mari Hersh-Tudor's "A Wilder Truth," another outsider, a changeling, is ostracized by her family and forced to make her way in the world.

The trauma, discomfort and fear brought on by puberty has its counterpart in the physical changes wrought by menopause. In

Barbara Ferrenz's "The Change," Karen seeks the help of a doctor to deal with depression. "Given your age," he advises, "we have to start thinking about the possibility of menopause." He sets forth a course of treatment that alters the future for both of them. To bring us full-circle from tales of pre-pubescence is Pamela J. Jessen's "Visitation," a nursing-home tale of a woman who reflects back on her life spent running with wolves.

Midway between these life-defining moments, the primitive power of the werewolf shines. In *"Euphorbia Helioscopia,"* Jeremy E. Johnson writes of an escape into the wild that encompasses both the great outdoors and the inner recesses of the heart. In "The Final Truth," Steve Eller, too, writes about an escape that strips Justin, a computer junkie, of his technological civilization and irrevocably ties him to the ancient world of the archetypal she-wolf. In a similar way, the waitress in Judy Brewer's "Moon Running" must confront the tension between her workaday relationships and her fear of her own primal secret.

Fear is at the heart of much of werewolf legend and folklore—fear of change, of the unknown, of inexplicable behavior, fear of strangers, a fear of what lurks deep within each of us. In Ursula K. Le Guin's "The Wife's Story," a mother fears for her children's safety around an unpredictable father, while in Melanie Tem's "Wilding," a tale of child abuse repeated generation after generation, Lydia fears her mother and grandmother as much as she fears her own desire.

When women are werewolves, it is through transformation that they come into their power. Such power is evident in Charlee Jacob's "Permafrost," in which one woman's freedom is another woman's fear. In "The Hound of God," by Tom Piccirilli, the werewolf is an ancestral guardian, her profound strength linked to and tempered by those with whom she lives. In Paul Allen's "Teamwork," Gretchen finds that her lost ability can now be found...but at a price.

As with so much horror, there is also a tradition of humor in the stories of werewolves. Animal magnetism is the basis for Renée M. Charles' "A Model of Transformation," a sleek send-up in which lupine beauty Tiarna takes the fashion world by storm. "Sisters of the Weird," Thomas S. Roche's tale of sisterhood, is a tongue-in-cheek celebration of marginality, freedom and individuality.

Whether bestial or gentle, murderous or chivalrous, the werewolf has always represented an inner-self, a soul if you will. And it is this definition of the werewolf that finds its counterpart in the Wild Woman that Estés encourages women to embrace in order to become complete human beings. Embracing the she-wolf within, however, carries another kind of risk as well. Joan Crawford put it perfectly in her closing remarks in the 1939 comic drama *The Women:* "There's a name for you ladies, but it isn't used in high society outside a kennel." The association of socially unacceptable female behavior with the behavior of wolves, dogs, and other canine creatures is really quite familiar.

Being a bitch is not something nice girls are taught to aspire to. Even so, when we look inside and release our anger, our rage, our desire, our need, the risk of being called a bitch is always right around the corner, the word always on the tip of someone's tongue. Whether we release our rage or keep it tightly bound, the potential to become what society fears and despises is always with us. As Estés reminds us, "No matter where we are, the shadow that trots behind us is definitely four-footed."

Bibliography

Baring-Gould, Sabine. *The Book of Werewolves.* Smit, Elder and Co. London, England. 1865.

Bush, Laurence. "She Bequeathed Them Her Claws..." *The Scream Factory. Special Werewolf Issue. #15,* Autumn 1994. pp. 8-14.

Cavendish, Richard. "Werewolf." *Man, Myth & Magic: The Illustrated Encyclopedia of Mythology, Religion and the Unknown.* Marshall Cavendish Corp. North Bellmore, NY. 1995. pp. 2779-2783.

Douglas, Adam. *The Beast Within: A History of the Werewolf.* Avon Books, NY. 1992.

Dziemianowicz, Stefan. "The Horror Pulpit." *The Scream Factory: Special Werewolf Issue. #15,* Autumn 1994. pp. 15-21.

Estés, Clarissa Pinkola. *Women Who Run with the Wolves: Myths and Stories of the Wild Woman Archetype.* Ballantine Books, NY. 1992.

Graham, Nancy. *Werewolves.* J.B. Lippincott and Co., Philadelphia. 1973.

McCallum, Lawrence. "Men into Wolves: The History of Lycanthropic Lore on the Movie Screen." *The Scream Factory. Special Werewolf Issue. #15,* Autumn 1994. pp. 64-73.

Storni, Alfonsina. *Selected Poems.* White Pine Press, NY. 1987.

Sullivan, Jack. "Werewolf." *The Penguin Encyclopedia of Horror and the Supernatural.* Viking Penguin, Inc. NY, NY. 1986. pp. 453-455.

Walker, Barbara G. *The Woman's Encyclopedia of Myths and Secrets.* Harper Collins, NY. 1983.

Permafrost

Charlee Jacob

The park tundra I run in is full of pine and birch. Running through the trees, I can see the sere alpine desert that rings this valley in a high white. Ice against my paws, numbing if I don't keep moving, exhilarating to cross at high speed. My thick fur is glacial silver; my eyes are a borealis blue. I have a flavor on my tongue as raw as the wind and as red as the blossoms on the Arctic lichen.

I raise my head and howl at the moon. This is what wolves do.

Shift. Move. Shake my head groggily. The lithium is toning down the euphoria of this episode. Bipolar disorder—what a term considering the cold landscape. The forest floor, soft with needles and leaves, is really torn matting. The high white desert, only the walls of this hospital room. The moon is the blazing light they hang over me so I rarely sleep. A manic/depressive.

I was being acute, running on all fours in an ever-tightening circle, gnashing my teeth, alive in the frigid mist, taking the delight in winter that only a good run can give in the biting northern air, tasting....

Raw and red. I bit the hand that fed me. The one with the syringe. Served him right. He cupped my teat and called me a little bitch. Wolf humor.

I have been here for three weeks, and they insist on that damned round, white light. Hoping I will believe it is the moon and change, so they can see me do it. Hoping I will not, so they can show me that I am not what I know myself to be.

Bring on the real moon. The soft ass, shining mother. I lean toward her, beckoning with my own ass, my own swelling breasts. I want to take a bite, want to lick her, want to jump over her. I want to land there so I can run through those valleys that look so inviting and into those mountains where the game must be most succulent. But the lithium and I fall back to earth together before I ever get far enough into space in my pelt, fall back to see these human hands and the droplets of milk on the nipples of these hairless breasts. Tasting only the blood where I bit my own tongue. The depression sets in, as it does for any animal who absolutely must run to be what she is, but who is restrained. The beast-will sedated into an unnatural hibernation.

The doctor comes in, frowning at the corner where I defecated.

"How is it that there are rat bones in your shit?" she asks me, perplexed.

"You didn't study much zoology in college, did you?" I smile and go over to it, poking my fingers into it to dislodge some of the bones. They have been well chewed. Marrow is good: tasty and healthy to ingest. "Indeed, the bones came from a rodent, but this wasn't a rat. It was a rabbit."

"How did you come by a rabbit in here?" Dr. Carson asks.

I remember. The hare was as snowy as the ground it raced across. My range of vision narrowed as I plunged after it, into a thin corridor of winter with only this rabbit at its center. The corridor grew narrower still until it became only a glowing streak of mercury ribbon supporting a fleeing animal. I panted and growled, and then I leapt.

Looking around now, I see the white walls/the high mountains/the alpine desert. I see the torn cotton batting on which baby bunting bunny died. I see the light that impersonates the carnal, loving, wooing moon but isn't she. I know the rabbit didn't die here, was never here at all. But its bones are. And its blood still coats my tongue. I stick it out and show Dr. Carson.

"You've bitten yourself again, Lisia" is all she says.

"Where did the bones come from then?" I spit the blood in her face. "Taste it. You might like it. You have a wolf in you, too, if only you would reach inside yourself and stroke her shaggy head."

Dr. Carson wipes the blood from her face, and I see her sniffing her fingers as she leaves. They come for me on her orders. I am led to The Room. I am put on the table and strapped down: plug in/bite down/go blank. This is the electro-convulsive vena cava. They use a forestful of needles to mellow out the fearshits and to dry up the saliva so I won't strangle. Atropine is alright even if I don't like the aftertaste. It is the essence of deadly nightshade that grows in niches of the loftiest rocks, blossoms ghostly faces even on moonless nights. Of course, those such as I are never concerned with nights when there is no moon.

The switch is thrown. I separate like an egg, my human self cringing in the darkness as my wolf self spins, baying, away from me. Shadows pass but I don't know them. All of space is filled with moons: memory lunas shooting by in round, black crusts. They are burning them! Blackened lumps pass me like the roasted shells of stars, robbed of their perfume; their crater vulvas and dusty, plain stomachs charred beyond distinction. I am an orphan of the thunder, a cub whose mother moon has been murdered by hunters. I must find myself in these orbs moving beyond me. I reach out and burn my hands on one of them. I shrink back. Another is wet and smells of garlic. It must be a meteorite, not a moon. I feel another trembling, a howling in keeping with the melancholy that promises to wrench me from this oblivion. I latch on fast. It cracks apart and my wolf head pushes through like it is being born, licking my face.

They have unstrapped me. I open my eyes after a long time passes and see Dr. Carson's face above me. She is a very pale woman. She has light green eyes with flecks of amber in them. Her breasts are small and high. I hear her heart beating as I sit up. I open my clenched fist and show her what is in my hand.

"Where did you get that?" she asks.

I grin. The shock with its infernal buzzing knocked out one of my teeth. I have a prominent gap in my strong, white human teeth. The tooth in my hand is a trenchant fang, bloody at the roots from having been dislodged during the ECT. She picks it up gingerly as if she is afraid to touch it.

"This isn't a human tooth. It isn't your tooth," she says.

"Do you ever dream of running in the snow, Doctor?"

I am taken back to my room. They give me a meal I cannot possibly eat. Then I am permitted to go to sleep. For once, I do.

The horizon is wide. The rocks that border the sky are ice-scratched, appearing as runes of mystery. I smell the moss, which has the green scent of primeval verdancy. The very first things to grow after the initial melting of the great ice age smelled like this. Rich, slippery, sexy: the pelt of a shifting world. The bristle-cone pine trees I see are denuded, a stripped scrollwork of bark reaches up along arms of bone. I also see a reindeer, sleek, shivering as it catches my scent, its flanks tightening in bounding leaps across the sedges. Which is better? The run or the kill or the feeding?

Always the run. Over the nearly frozen waters that scream as they race foaming over the breaks, shattering ice crystals under our bellies as we sail over them. Down the slopes and into ground willow. The struggle in a meadow of alpine lilies where the running stops but the body is still at full tilt, adrenalin pumping through the mesh of muscles. Our brains pop cells of northern lights.

I hear an orderly cry out. I see that damned imposter moon overhead, not my soothing lover moon. I drowse, luxuriating in the sticky wash, stretching my slender human legs again. I have one lithely muscled arm draped across the carcass, I look up impishly as Dr. Carson hurries in, staring at me, staring at the reindeer with its throat torn open, its tongue lolling, its eyes gone to glass, meat taken in chunks from its underbelly.

"How...?" she stammers.

Somehow I have stripped myself of the cumbersome restraint they fitted me with some hours before. I am naked and glorious, smeared in gore from head to foot as if I crawled inside the deer, swam in its salty waters under sheens of lake-ice until I found the frost-smoke heart and then emerged again shaking ephemeral ice flowers from my whiskers. My hair is red. I don't even remember what color my hair usually is.

But there is more. The reindeer's coat is covered with snow. There are damp paw prints with snow still bunched between the clawmarks. On the floor, up the walls, across the ceiling. Snow is melting from between the bloody prints of toes and fingers. A film of snow coats my eyelashes. I see the doctor and the stupid orderly through a silver haze.

"This is a hallucination," Dr. Carson says firmly.

"Yours or mine?" I ask, posing prettily. The orderly ogles as I spread my legs. I close them again and growl at him.

"Robert, get some help in here and remove this deer," she orders.

"This is mine," I tell her. "Get your own."

I lift my head and howl, uncannily, throaty, a music of spheres of the moon, a ballad to its phases.

The hospital walls begin shaking as the patients in other rooms scream with the echo of my voice. Some are even howling too. Warning buzzers are going off at all the nurses' stations and Dr. Carson's beeper goes off at her hip. The spot of hot, white light on my ceiling goes out.

They don't call it bedlam for nothing.

I hear the doctor gasp.

"Don't be afraid. It's only an eclipse," I explain. "Simulate the moon and you may get her idiosyncrasies. It will pass."

But I never said I wouldn't touch her, thinking in my mind that this was not anything the doctor need fear. I rub blood across her cheeks, down her chin with an icy finger, a line of it down her throat gently, under her coat and between her pearly breasts.

"Please step back, Lisia," she commands, but her voice quavers. The smell of blood may have this effect.

The noise all over the hospital is tremendous. Voices from every room—even from the catatonics—rise in a manic chant that can only be described as painfully ancient. The cave people and the hunter/gatherers made such sounds as they watched the glaciers come in and sail away in placid harbors, watching the ice crumble, watching it climb to the stars.

"There really is a full moon tonight, isn't there?" I ask, not having been near a window in more than three weeks.

She admits it.

"Take me to it," I whisper seductively. "If you really want to know, then take me to any opening, door or window. You will have no more questions. Not about anything."

Dr. Carson leads me in the dark from my cell, from the sanctum that can no longer fool me. I have fooled it. Her light green eyes with their yellow flecks almost glow.

People in those lackluster white uniforms are running pell-mell, shouting orders to shut down this and that ward, demanding more ultrashort-acting barbituates, restraint belts, even the old-style straightjackets and wire muzzles that institutions don't use anymore but are still kept in the cellar. I see a nurse sitting in a corner, pounding out a curious rhythm on a bed pan, her hair pulled from the starched cap and tight bun to hang in her face like a shaman's greasy locks. Another has a tray of ice and is inserting the cubes into her vagina one at a time.

"I'm afraid I must take you back to your room, Lisia. I am needed here, it seems," Dr. Carson says, seeing the misrule that has erupted.

I grab her arm.

"There are seldom moments of truth for any of us, Doctor. Here is one. You've locked me up as insane, but I know you've wondered. Certainty is the gift of night, Doctor, of *this* night. Let it pass and it will be gone forever."

She steers me to a door that leads to the garden where on sunny days certain ambulatory patients are allowed to vegetate among the rose bushes. Sometimes they read tarot cards or play chess with figures carved from terra cotta to resemble the creatures painted on prehistoric cave walls. There is no one out there now, of course. It is dark; it is black. She shuts the door behind us.

There is an eclipse. The moon-lover is an ebony disk. She is hiding and playing lovers' games. I still smell her, though, for no darkness can secret her musk. I feel a rumble building in the back of my throat, husky and aroused.

"You see well in the dark, Doctor," I say.

We listen as the people inside shriek and bay in turns, as the glass in what few windows there are begins to crack. There is a spray of rose petals, arterial red. The moon of unending *fimbul-vetr* and voracious snow maidens returns.

The garden changes abruptly. It is an ice-floe, a great glacier projecting up beneath us, carrying us upward, inexorably forward. Dr. Carson staggers and I catch her in my arms, helping her get her footing as the iceberg roars with radiant showers of crystals all around us. The temperature has dropped forty, fifty, sixty degrees and she is shivering. Our breath as we exhale forms fantasy archipelagoes that drift through the air. The ice crackles as if electric, hums from the hollows being created and then filled by its bulk.

Dr. Carson turns to me, terror in her eyes. I open my mouth and she sees the icicles. She feels them in her mouth, growing from her fingertips.

I hold my hands up to show her the deep, rich silver fur.

"Soon we will be warm enough, as long as we begin to run and keep on running," I tell her. She starts to scream, but all that comes out is a feral yowl. She extends it, singing to the moon.

"Where has the moon gone?" she asks, ears flattening back with alarm against her vulpine skull. I gesture to the sere luna desert all around, the icy dust in this tranquil valley of high white.

"We are riding her," I reply, my smile brimming with permafrost.

Boobs

Suzy McKee Charnas

The thing is, it's like your brain wants to go on thinking about the miserable History midterm you have tomorrow, but your body takes over. And what a body! You can see in the dark and run like the wind and leap parked cars in a single bound.

Of course, you pay for it the next morning (but it's worth it). I always wake up stiff and sore, with dirty hands and feet and face, and I have to jump in the shower fast so Hilda won't see me like that.

Not that she would know what it was about, but why take chances? So I pretend it's the other thing that's bothering me. So she goes, "Come on, sweetie, everybody gets cramps; that's no reason to go around moaning and groaning. What are you doing, trying to get out of school just because you have your period?"

If I didn't like Hilda, which I do even though she is only a step-mother instead of my real mother, I would show her something that would keep me out of school forever, and it's not fake either.

But there are plenty of people I'd rather show that to.

I already showed that dork Billy Linden.

"Hey, Boobs!" he goes, in the hall right outside Homeroom. A lot of kids laughed, naturally, though Rita Frye called him an asshole.

Billy is the one that started it, sort of, because he always started everything, him and his big mouth. At the beginning of the term, he came barrelling down on me hollering, "Hey, look at Bornstein, something musta happened to her over the summer! What happened, Bornstein? Hey, everybody, look at Boobs Bornstein!"

He made a grab at my chest, and I socked him in the shoulder, and he punched me in the face, which made me dizzy and shocked and made me cry, too, in front of everybody.

I mean, I always used to wrestle and fight with the boys, being

25

that I was strong for a girl. All of a sudden it was different. He hit me hard, to really hurt me, and the shock sort of got me in the pit of my stomach and made me feel nauseous, too, as well as mad and embarrassed to death.

I had to go home with a bloody nose and lie with my head back and ice wrapped in a towel on my face and dripping down into my hair.

Hilda sat on the couch next to me and patted me. She goes, "I'm sorry about this, honey, but really, you have to learn it sometime. You're all growing up and the boys are getting stronger than you'll ever be. If you fight with boys, you're bound to get hurt. You have to find other ways to handle them."

To make things worse, the next morning I started to bleed down there, which Hilda had explained carefully to me a couple of times, so at least I knew what was going on. Hilda really tried extra hard without being icky about it, but I hated when she talked about how it was all part of these exciting changes in my body that are so important and how terrific it is "to become a young woman."

Sure. The whole thing was so messy and disgusting, worse than she had said, worse than I could imagine, with these black clots of gunk coming out in a smear of pink blood—I thought I would throw up. That's just the lining of your uterus, Hilda said. Big deal. It was still gross.

And plus, the *smell*.

Hilda tried to make me feel better, she really did. She said we should "mark the occasion" like primitive people do, so it's something special, not just a nasty thing that just sort of falls on you.

So we decided to put poor old Pinkie away, my stuffed dog that I've slept with since I was three. Pinkie is bald and sort of hard and lumpy, since he got put in the washing machine by mistake, and you would never know he was all soft plush when he was new, or even that he was pink.

Last time my friend Gerry-Anne came over, before the summer, she saw Pinky lying on my pillow and though she didn't say anything, I could tell she was thinking that was kind of babyish. So I'd been thinking about not keeping Pinky around any more.

Hilda and I made him this nice box lined with pretty scraps from her quilting class, and I thanked him out loud for being my friend for so many years, and we put him up in the closet on the top shelf.

I felt terrible, but if Gerry-Anne decided I was too babyish to be friends with any more, I could end up with no friends at all. When you have never been popular since the time you were skinny and fast and everybody wanted you on their team, you have that kind of thing on your mind.

Hilda and Dad made me go to school the next morning so nobody would think that I was scared of Billy Linden (which I was) or that I would let him keep me away just by being such a dork.

Everybody kept sneaking funny looks at me and whispering, and I was sure it was because I couldn't help walking funny with the pad between my legs and because they could smell what was happening, which as far as I knew hadn't happened to anyone else in Eight A yet. Just like nobody else in the whole grade had anything real in their stupid training bras except me, thanks a lot.

Anyway, I stayed away from everybody as much as I could and wouldn't talk to Gerry-Anne, even, because I was scared she would ask me why I walked funny and smelled bad.

Billy Linden avoided me just like everybody else, except one of his stupid buddies purposely bumped into me so I stumbled into Billy on the lunchline. Billy turns around and he goes, real loud, "Hey, Boobs, when did you start wearing black and blue makeup?"

I didn't give him the satisfaction of knowing that he had actually broken my nose, which the doctor said. Good thing they don't have to bandage you up for that. Billy would be hollering up a storm about how I had my nose in a sling as well as my boobs.

That night I got up after I was supposed to be asleep and took off my underpants and T-shirt that I sleep in and stood looking at myself in the mirror. I didn't need to turn a light on. The moon was full, and it was shining right into my bedroom through the big dormer window.

I crossed my arms and pinched myself hard to sort of punish my body for what it was doing to me.

As if I could make it stop.

No wonder Edie Siler had starved herself to death in the tenth grade! I understood her perfectly. She was trying to keep her body down, keep it normal-looking, thin and strong, like I was too, back when I looked like a person, not a cartoon that somebody would call "Boobs."

And then something warm trickled in a little line down the inside of my leg, and I knew it was blood and I couldn't stand it any more. I pressed my thighs together and shut my eyes hard, and I did something.

I mean I felt it happening. I felt myself shrink down to a hard core of sort of cold fire inside my bones, and all the flesh part, the muscles and the squishy insides and the skin, went sort of glowing and free-floating, all shining with moonlight, and I felt a sort of shifting and balance-changing going on.

I thought I was fainting on account of my stupid period. So I turned around and threw myself on my bed, only by the time I hit it, I knew something was seriously wrong.

For one thing, my nose and my head were crammed with these crazy, rich sensations that took me a second to even figure out were smells, they were so much stronger than any smells I'd ever smelled. And they were—I don't know—*interesting* instead of just stinky, even the rotten ones.

I opened my mouth to get the smells a little better, and heard myself panting in a funny way as if I'd been running, which I hadn't, and then there was this long part of my face sticking out and something moving there—my tongue.

I was licking my chops.

Well, there was this moment of complete and utter panic. I tore around the room whining and panting and hearing my toenails clicking on the floorboards, and then I huddled down and crouched in the corner because I was scared Dad and Hilda would hear me and come to find out what was making all this racket.

Because I could hear them. I could hear their bed creak when one of them turned over, and Dad's breath whistling a little in an almost snore, and I could smell them too, each one with a perfectly clear bunch of smells, kind of like those desserts of mixed ice cream they call a medley.

My body was twitching and jumping with fear and energy, and my room—a converted attic space, wide but with a ceiling that's low in places—my room felt like a jail. And plus, I was terrified of catching a glimpse of myself in the mirror. I had a pretty good idea of what I would see, and I didn't want to see it.

Besides, I had to pee, and I couldn't face trying to deal with the toilet in the state I was in.

So I eased the bedroom door open with my shoulder and nearly fell down the stairs trying to work them with four legs and thinking about it, instead of letting my body just do it. I put my hands on the front door to open it, but my hands weren't hands, they were paws with long knobby toes covered with fur, and the toes had thick black claws sticking out of the ends of them.

The pit of my stomach sort of exploded with horror, and I yelled. It came out this wavery "wooo" noise that echoed eerily in my skull-bones. Upstairs, Hilda goes, "Jack, what was that?" I bolted for the basement as I heard Dad hit the floor of their bedroom.

The basement door slips its latch all the time, so I just shoved it open and down I went, doing better on the stairs this time because I was too scared to think. I spent the rest of the night down there, moaning to myself (which meant whining through my nose, really) and trotting around rubbing against the walls trying to rub off this crazy shape I had, or just moving around because I couldn't sit still. The place was thick with stinks and these slow-swirling currents of hot and cold air. I couldn't handle all the input.

As for having to pee, in the end I managed to sort of hike my butt up over the edge of the slop-sink by Dad's workbench and let go in there. The only problem was that I couldn't turn the taps on to rinse out the smell because of my paws.

Then about three a.m. I woke up from a doze curled up in a bare place on the floor where the spiders weren't so likely to walk, and I couldn't see a thing or smell anything either, so I knew I was okay again even before I checked and found fingers on my hands instead of claws.

I zipped upstairs and stood under the shower so long that Hilda yelled at me for using up the hot water when she had a load of wash to do that morning. I was only trying to steam some of the stiffness out of my muscles, but I couldn't tell her that.

It was real weird to just dress and go to school after a night like that. One good thing, I had stopped bleeding after only one day, which Hilda said wasn't so strange for the first time. So it had to be the huge greenish bruise on my face from Billy's punch that every-one was staring at.

That and the usual thing, of course. Well, why not? *They* didn't know I'd spent the night as a wolf.

So Fat Joey grabbed my book bag in the hallway outside science class and tossed it to some kid from Eight B. I had to run after them to get it back, which of course was set up so the boys could cheer the jouncing of my boobs under my shirt.

I was so mad I almost caught Fat Joey, except I was afraid if I grabbed him, maybe he would sock me like Billy had.

Dad had told me, Don't let it get you, kid, all boys are jerks at that age.

Hilda had been saying all summer, Look, it doesn't do any good to walk around all hunched up with your arms crossed, you should just throw your shoulders back and walk like a proud person who's pleased that she's growing up. You're just a little early, that's all, and I bet the other girls are secretly envious of you, with their cute little training bras, for Chrissake, as if there was something that needed to be *trained.*

It's okay for her, she's not in school, she doesn't remember what it's like.

So I quit running and walked after Joey until the bell rang, and then I got my bag back from the bushes outside where he threw it. I was crying a little, and I ducked into the girls' room.

Stacey Buhl was in there doing her lipstick like usual and wouldn't talk to me like usual, but Rita came bustling in and said somebody should off that dumb dork Joey, except of course, it was really Billy that had put him up to it. Like usual.

Rita is okay except she's an outsider herself, being that her kid brother has AIDS, and lots of kids' parents don't think she should even be in the school. So I don't hang around with her a lot. I've got enough trouble, and anyway I was late for Math.

I had to talk to somebody, though. After school I told Gerry-Anne, who's been my best friend on and off since fourth grade. She was off at the moment, but I found her in the library and I told her I'd had a weird dream about being a wolf. She wants to be a psychiatrist like her mother, so of course she listened.

She told me I was nuts. That was a big help.

That night I made sure the back door wasn't exactly closed, and then I got in bed with no clothes on—imagine turning into a wolf in your underpants and T-shirt—and just shivered waiting for something to happen.

The moon came up and shone in my window, and I changed again, just like before, which is not one bit like how it is in the movies—all struggling and screaming and bones snapping out with horrible cracking and tearing noises, just the way I guess you would imagine it to be, if you knew it had to be done by building special machines to do that for the camera and make it look real: if you were a special-effects man, instead of a werewolf.

For me, it didn't have to look real, it was real. It was this melting and drifting thing, which I got sort of excited by this time. I mean it felt—interesting. Like something I was doing, instead of just another dumb body-mess happening to me because some brainless hormones said so.

I must have made a noise. Hilda came upstairs to the door of my bedroom, but luckily she didn't come in. She's tall, and my ceiling is low for her, so she often talks to me from the landing.

Anyway I'd heard her coming, so I was in my bed with my whole head shoved under my pillow, praying frantically that nothing showed.

I could smell her, it was the wildest thing—her own smell, sort of sweaty but sweet, and then on top if it her perfume, like an ice-pick stuck in my nose. I didn't actually hear a word she said, I was too scared, and also I had this ripply shaking feeling inside me, a high that was only partly terror.

See, I realized all of a sudden, with this big blossom of surprise, that I didn't have to be scared of Hilda, or anybody. I was strong, my wolf-body was strong, and anyhow, one clear look at me and she would drop dead.

What a relief, though, when she went away. I was dying to get out from under the weight of the covers, and besides I had to sneeze. Also, I recognized that part of the energy roaring around inside me was hunger.

They went to bed—I heard their voices even in their bedroom, though not exactly what they said, which was fine. The words weren't important anymore, I could tell more from the tone of what they were saying.

Like I knew they were going to do it, and I was right. I could hear them messing around right through the walls, which was also something new, and I have never been so embarrassed in my life. I couldn't even put my hands over my ears, because my hands were paws.

So while I was waiting for them to go to sleep, I looked myself over in the big mirror on my closet door.

There was this big wolf head with a long slim muzzle and a thick ruff around my neck. The ruff stood up as I growled and backed up a little.

Which was silly of course, because there was no wolf in the bedroom. But I was all strung out, I guess, and one wolf, me in my wolf body, was as much as I could handle, let alone the idea of two wolves, me and my reflection.

After that first shock, it was great. I kept turning one way and another for different views.

I was thin, with these long, slender legs but strong, you could see the muscles, and feet a little bigger than I would have picked. But I'll take four big feet over two big boobs any day.

My face was terrific, with jaggedy white ripsaw teeth and eyes that were small and clear and gleaming in the moonlight. The tail was a little bizarre, but I got used to it, and actually it had a nice plumy shape. My shoulders were big and covered with long, glossy-looking fur, and I had this neat coloring, dark on the back and a sort of melting silver on my front and underparts.

The thing was, though, my tongue was hanging out. I had a lot of trouble with that, it looked gross and silly at the same time. I mean, that was *my tongue*, about a foot long and neatly draped over the points of my bottom canines. That was when I realized that I didn't have a whole lot of expressions to use, not with that face, which was more like a mask.

But it was alive, it was my face, those were my own long black lips that my tongue licked.

No doubt about it, this was me. I was a werewolf, like in the movies they showed over Halloween weekend. But it wasn't anything like your ugly movie werewolf that's just some guy loaded up with pounds and pounds of makeup. I was *gorgeous*.

I didn't want to just hang around admiring myself in the mirror, though. I couldn't stand being cooped up in that stuffy, smell-crowded room.

When everything settled down and I could hear Dad and Hilda breathing the way they do when they're sleeping, I snuck out.

The dark wasn't very dark to me, and the cold felt sharp like vinegar, but not in a hurting way. Everyplace I went, there were these currents like waves in the air, and I could draw them in through my long wolf nose and roll the smell of them over the back of my tongue. It was like a whole different world, with bright sounds everywhere and rich, strong smells.

And I could run.

I started running because a car came by while I was sniffing at the garbage bags on the curb, and I was really scared of being seen in the headlights. So I took off down the dirt alley between our house and the Morrisons' next door, and holy cow, I could tear along with hardly a sound, I could jump their picket fence without even thinking about it. My back legs were like steel springs and I came down solid and square on four legs with almost no shock at all, let alone worrying about losing my balance or twisting an ankle.

Man, I could run through that chilly air all thick and moisty with smells, I could almost fly. It was like last year, when I didn't have boobs bouncing and yanking in front even when I'm only walking fast.

Just two rows of neat little bumps down the curve of my belly. I sat down and looked.

I tore open garbage bags to find out about the smells in them, but I didn't eat anything from them. I wasn't about to chow down on other people's stale hotdog-ends and pizza crusts and fat and bones scraped off their plates and all mixed up with mashed potatoes and stuff.

When I found places where dogs had stopped and made their mark, I squatted down and pissed there too, right on top, I just wiped them out.

I bounded across that enormous lawn around the Wanscombe place, where nobody but the Oriental gardener ever sets foot, and walked up the back and over the top of their BMW, leaving big fat pawprints all over it. Nobody saw me, nobody heard me, I was a shadow.

Well, except for the dogs, of course.

There was a lot of barking when I went by, real hysterics, which at first really scared me. But then I popped out of an alley up on Ridge Road, where the big houses are, right in front of about six dogs that run together. Their owners let them out all night and don't care if they get hit by a car.

They'd been trotting along with the wind behind them, checking out all the garbage bags set out for pick-up the next morning. When they saw me, one of them let out a yelp of surprise, and they all skidded to a stop.

Six of them. I was scared. I growled.

The dogs turned fast, banging into each other in their hurry, and trotted away.

I don't know what they would have done if they met a real wolf, but I was something special, I guess.

I followed them.

They scattered and ran.

Well, I ran too, and this was a different kind of running. I mean, I stretched, and I raced, and there was this joy. I chased one of them.

Zig, zag, this little terrier kind of dog tried to cut left and dive under the gate of somebody's front walk, all without a sound—he was running too hard to yell, and I was happy running quiet.

Just before he could ooze under the gate, I caught up with him and without thinking I grabbed the back of his neck and pulled him off his feet and gave him a shake as hard as I could, from side to side.

I felt his neck crack, the sound vibrated through all the bones of my face.

I picked him up in my mouth, and it was like he hardly weighed a thing. I trotted away holding him up off the ground, and under a bush in Baker's Park I held him down with my paws and I bit into his belly, which was still warm and quivering.

Like I said, I was hungry.

The blood gave me this rush like you wouldn't believe. I stood there a minute looking around and licking my lips, just sort of panting and tasting the taste because I was stunned by it, it was like eating honey or the best chocolate malted you ever had.

So I put my head down and chomped that little dog, like shoving your face into a pizza and inhaling it. God, I was *starved,* so I didn't mind that the meat was tough and rank-tasting after that first wonderful bite. I even licked blood off the ground after, never mind the grit mixed in.

I ate two more dogs that night, one that was tied up on a clothesline in a cruddy yard full of rusted-out car parts down on the South side, and one fat old yellow dog out snuffling around on his own and way too slow. He tasted pretty bad, and by then I was feeling full, so I left a lot.

I strolled around the park, shoving the swings with my big black wolf nose, and I found the bench where Mr. Granby sits and feeds the pigeons every day, never mind that nobody else wants the dirty birds around crapping on their cars. I took a dump there, right where he sits.

Then I gave the setting moon a goodnight, which came out quavery and wild, "Loo-loo-loo!" And I loped toward home, springing off the thick pads of my paws and letting my tongue loll out and feeling generally super.

I slipped inside and trotted upstairs, and in my room I stopped to look at myself in the mirror.

As gorgeous as before, and only a few dabs of blood on me, which I took time to lick off. I did get a little worried—I mean, suppose that was it, suppose having killed and eaten in my wolf shape, I was stuck in this shape forever? Like, if you wander into a fairy castle and eat or drink anything, that's it, you can't ever leave. Suppose when the morning came I didn't change back?

Well, there wasn't much I could do about that one way or the other, and to tell the truth, I felt like I wouldn't mind; it had been worth it.

When I was nice and clean, having even licked off my own bottom, which seemed like a perfectly normal and nice thing to do at the time, I jumped up on the bed, curled up, and corked right off. When I woke up with the sun in my eyes, there I was, my own self again.

It was very strange, grabbing breakfast and wearing my old sweat-shirt that wallowed all over me so I didn't stick out so much, while Hilda yawned and shuffled around in her robe and slippers and acted like she and Dad hadn't been doing it last night, which I knew different.

And plus, it was perfectly clear that she didn't have a clue about what I had been doing, which gave me a strange feeling.

One of the things about growing up that they're careful not to tell you is you start having more things you don't talk to your parents about. And I had a doozie.

Hilda goes, "What's the matter, are you off Sugar Pops now? Honestly, Kelsey, I can't keep up with you! And why can't you wear something nicer than that old shirt to school? Oh, I get it: disguise, right?"

She sighed and looked at me kind of sad but smiling, her hands on her hips. "Kelsey, Kelsey," she goes, "if only I'd had half of what you've got when I was a girl—I was flat as an ironing board, and it made me so miserable, I can't tell you."

She's still real thin and neat-looking, so what does she know about it? But she meant well, and anyhow I was feeling so good I didn't argue.

I didn't change my shirt, though.

That night I didn't turn into a wolf. I lay there waiting, but though the moon came up, nothing happened no matter how hard I tried, and after a while I went and looked out the window and realized that the moon wasn't really full any more, it was getting smaller.

I wasn't so much relieved as sorry. I bought a calendar at the school book sale two weeks later, and I checked the full moon nights coming up and waited anxiously to see what would happen.

Meantime, things rolled along as usual. I got a rash of zits on my chin. I would look in the mirror and think about my wolf-face, which had beautiful sleek fur instead of zits.

Zits and all, I went to Angela Durkin's party, and the next day Billy Linden told everybody that I went in one of the bedrooms at Angela's and made out with him, which I did not. But since no grown-ups were home and Fat Joey brought grass to the party, most of the kids were stoned and didn't know who did what or where anyhow.

As a matter of fact, Billy once actually did get a girl in Seven B high one time out in his parents' garage, and him and two of his friends did it to her while she was zonked out of her mind, or any way they said they did, and she was too embarrassed to say anything one way or the other, and a little while later she changed schools.

How I know about it is the same way everybody else does, because Billy was the biggest boaster in the whole school, and you could never tell if he was lying or not.

So I guess it wasn't so surprising that some people believed what Billy said about me. Gerry-Anne quit talking to me after that. Meantime Hilda got pregnant.

This turned into a huge discussion about how Hilda had been worried about her biological clock so she and Dad had decided to have a kid, and I shouldn't mind, it would be fun for me and good preparation for being a mother myself later on, when I found some nice guy and got married.

Sure. Great preparation. Like Mary O'Hare in my class, who gets to change her youngest baby sister's diapers all the time, yick. She jokes about it, but you can tell she really hates it. Now it looked like my turn was coming up, as usual.

The only thing that made life bearable was my secret.

"You're laid back today," Devon Brown said to me in the lunch-room one day after Billy had been specially obnoxious, trying to flick rolled up pieces of bread from his table so they would land on my chest. Devon was sitting with me because he was bad at French, my only good subject, and I was helping him out with some verbs. I guess he wanted to know why I wasn't upset because of Billy picking on me. He goes, "Howcome?"

"That's a secret," I said, thinking about what Devon would say if he knew a werewolf was helping him with his French: *loup. Manger.*

He goes, "What secret?" Devon has freckles and is actually kind of cute-looking.

"A *secret*," I go, "so I can't tell you, dummy."

He looks real superior and he goes, "Well, it can't be much of a secret, because girls can't keep secrets, everybody knows that."

Sure, like that kid Sara in Eight B who it turned out her own father had been molesting for years, but she never told anybody until some psychologist caught on from some tests we all had to take in seventh grade. Up 'til then, Sara kept her secret fine.

And I kept mine, marking off the days on the calendar. The only part I didn't look forward to was having a period again, which last time came right before the change.

When the time came, I got crampy and more zits popped out on my face, but I didn't have a period.

I changed, though.

The next morning they were talking in school about a couple of prize miniature Schnauzers at the Wanscombes that had been hauled out of their yard by somebody and killed, and almost nothing left of them.

Well, my stomach turned a little when I heard some kids describing what Mr. Wanscombe had found over in Baker's Park, "the remains," as people said. I felt a little guilty, too, because Mr. Wanscombe had really loved those little dogs, which somehow I didn't think about at all when I was a wolf the night before, trotting around hungry in the moonlight.

I knew those Schnauzers personally, so I was sorry, even if they were irritating little mutts that made a lot of noise.

But heck, the Wanscombes shouldn't have left them out all night in the cold. Anyhow, they were rich, they could buy new ones if they wanted.

Still and all, though. I mean, dogs are just dumb animals. If they're mean, it's because they're wired that way or somebody made them mean, they can't help it. They can't just decide to be nice, like a person can. And plus, they don't taste so great, I think because they put so much junk in commercial dog foods—anti-worm medicine and ashes and ground-up fish, stuff like that. Ick.

In fact, after the second Schnauzer, I had felt sort of sick and didn't sleep real well that night. So I was not in a great mood to start with, and that was the day that my new brassiere disappeared while I was in gym. Later on I got passed a note telling me where to find it: stapled to the bulletin board outside the principal's office, where everybody could see that I was trying a bra with an underwire.

Naturally, it had to be Stacey Buhl that grabbed my bra while I was changing for gym and my back was turned, since she was now hanging around with Billy and his friends.

Billy went around all day making bets at the top of his lungs on how soon I would be wearing a D-cup.

Stacey didn't matter, she was just a jerk. Billy mattered. He had wrecked me in that school forever, with his nasty mind and his big, fat mouth. I was past crying or fighting or getting punched out. I was boiling, I had had enough crap from him, and I had an idea.

I followed Billy home and waited on his porch until his mom came home and she made him come down and talk to me. He stood in the doorway and talked through the screen door, eating a banana and lounging around like he didn't have a care in the world.

So he goes, "Whatcha want, Boobs?"

I stammered a lot, being that I was so nervous about telling such big lies, but that probably made me sound more believable.

I told him that I would make a deal with him: I would meet him that night in Baker's Park, late, and take off my shirt and bra and let him do whatever he wanted with my boobs if it would satisfy his curiosity and he would find somebody else to pick on and leave me alone.

"What?" he said, staring at my chest with his mouth open. His voice squeaked and he was practically drooling on the floor. He couldn't believe his good luck.

I said the same thing over again.

He almost came out onto the porch to try it right then and there. "Well, shit," he goes, lowering his voice a lot, "why didn't you say something before? You really mean it?"

I go, "Sure," though I couldn't look at him.

After a minute he goes, "Okay, it's a deal. Listen, Kelsey, if you like it, can we, uh, do it again, you know?"

I go, "Sure. But Billy, one thing: this is a secret, between just you

38

and me. If you tell anybody, if there's one other person hanging around out there tonight—"

"Oh no," he goes, real fast, "I won't say a thing to anybody, honest. Not a word, I promise!"

Not until afterward, of course, was what he meant, which if there was one thing Billy Linden couldn't do, it was to keep quiet if he knew something bad about another person.

"You're gonna like it, I know you are," he goes, speaking strictly for himself as usual. "Jeez. I can't believe this!"

But he did, the dork.

I couldn't eat much for dinner that night, I was too excited, so I told Dad and Hilda I was going upstairs early to do homework.

Then I waited for the moon, and when it came, I changed.

Billy was in the park. I caught a whiff of him, very sweaty and excited, but I stayed cool. I snuck around for a while, as quietly as I could—which was real quiet—making sure none of his stupid friends were lurking around. I mean, I wouldn't have trusted just his promise for a million dollars.

I passed up half a hamburger lying in the gutter where somebody had parked for lunch and eaten in their car next to Baker's Park. My mouth watered, but I didn't want to spoil my appetite. I was hungry and happy, sort of singing inside my own head, *"Shoo, fly, pie, and an apple-pan-dowdie..."*

Without any sound, of course.

Billy had been sitting on a bench, his hands in his pockets, twisting around to look this way and that way, watching for me—for my human self—to come join him. He had a jacket on since it was very chilly out.

He hadn't stopped to think that maybe a sane person wouldn't be crazy enough to sit out there and take off her top leaving her naked skin bare to the breeze. But that was Billy all right, totally fixed on his own greedy self without a single thought for somebody else. I bet all he could think about was what a great scam this was, to feel up old Boobs in the park and then crow about it all over school.

Now he was walking around the park, kicking at the sprinkler heads and glancing up every once in a while, frowning and looking sulky.

I could see that he was starting to think that I might stand him up. Maybe he even suspected that old Boobs was lurking around watching him and laughing to herself because he had fallen for a trick. Maybe old Boobs had even brought some kids from school with her to see what a jerk he was.

Actually that would have been pretty good, except Billy probably would have broken my nose again, or worse, if I'd tried it.

"Kelsey?" he goes, sounding mad.

I didn't want him stomping off home in a huff. I moved up closer, and I let the bushes swish a little around my shoulders.

He goes, "Hey, Kelse, it's late, where've you been?"

I listened to the words, but mostly I listened to the little thread of worry flickering in his voice, low and high, high and low, as he tried to figure out what was going on.

I let out the whisper of a growl.

He stood real still, staring at the bushes, and he goes, "That you, Kelse? Answer me."

I was wild inside, I couldn't wait another second. I tore through the bushes and leaped for him, flying.

He stumbled backward with a squawk—"What!"—jerking his hands up in front of his face, and he was just sucking in a big breath to yell with when I hit him like a demo-derby truck.

I jammed my nose past his feeble claws and chomped down hard on his face.

No sound came out of him except this wet, thick gurgle, which I could more taste than hear because the sound came right into my mouth with the gush of his blood and the hot mess of meat and skin that I tore away and swallowed.

He thrashed around, hitting at me, but I hardly felt anything through my fur. I mean, he wasn't so big and strong lying there on the ground with me, all lean and wiry wolf-muscle, straddling him. And plus, he was in shock. I got a strong whiff from below as he let go of everything right into his pants.

Dogs were barking, but so many people around Baker's Park have dogs to keep out burglars, and the dogs make such a racket all the time, that nobody pays any attention. I wasn't worried. Anyway, I was too busy to care.

I nosed in under what was left of Billy's jaw and I bit his throat out.

Now let him go around telling lies about people.

His clothes were a lot of trouble and I really missed having hands. I managed to drag his shirt out of his belt with my teeth, though, and it was easy to tear his belly open. Pretty messy, but once I got in there, it was better than Thanksgiving dinner. Who would think that somebody as horrible as Billy Linden could taste so *good?*

He was barely moving by then, and I quit thinking about him as Billy Linden any more. I quit thinking at all, I just pushed my head in and pulled out delicious steaming chunks and ate until I was picking at tidbits, and everything was getting cold.

On the way home I saw a police car cruising the neighborhood the way they do sometimes. I hid in the shadows and of course they never saw me.

There was a lot of washing up to do in the morning, and when Hilda saw my sheets she shook her head and she goes, "You should be more careful about keeping track of your period so as not to get caught by surprise."

Everybody in school knew something had happened to Bobby Linden, but it wasn't until the day after that that they got the word. Kids stood around in little huddles trading rumors about how some wild animal had chewed Billy up. I would walk up and listen in and add a really gross remark or two, like part of the game of thrilling each other green and nauseous with made-up details to see who would upchuck first.

Not me, that's for sure. I mean, when somebody went on about how Billy's whole head was gnawed down to the skull and they didn't even know who he was except for the bus pass in his wallet, I got a little urpy. It's amazing the things people will dream up. But when I thought about what I had actually done to Billy, I had to smile.

It felt totally wonderful to walk through the halls without having anybody yelling, "Hey, Boobs!"

There are people who just plain do not deserve to live. And the same goes for Fat Joey, if he doesn't quit crowding me in science lab, trying to get a feel.

One funny thing, though, I don't get periods at all any more. I get a little crampy, and my breasts get sore, and I break out more than usual—and then instead of bleeding, I change.

Which is fine with me, though I take a lot more care now about how I hunt on my wolf nights. I stay away from Baker's Park. The suburbs go on for miles and miles, and there are lots of places I can hunt and still get home by morning. A running wolf can cover a lot of ground.

And I make sure I make my kills where I can eat in private, so no cop car can catch me unawares, which could easily have happened that night when I killed Billy, I was so deep into the eating thing that first time. I look around a lot more now when I'm eating a kill, I keep watch.

Good thing it's only once a month that this happens, and only a couple of nights. "The Full Moon Killer" has the whole state up in arms and terrified as it is.

Eventually I guess I'll have to go somewhere else, which I'm not looking forward to at all. If I can just last until I have a car of my own, life will get a lot easier.

Meantime, some wolf nights I don't even feel like hunting. Mostly I'm not as hungry as I was those first times. I think I must have been storing up my appetite for a long time. Sometimes I just prowl around and I run, boy do I run.

If I am hungry, sometimes I eat from the garbage instead of killing somebody. It's no fun, but you do get a taste for it. I don't mind garbage as long as once in a while I can have the real thing fresh-killed, nice and wet. People can be awfully nasty, but they sure taste sweet.

I do pick and choose, though. I look for people sneaking around in the middle of the night, like Billy, waiting in the park that time. I figure they've got to be out looking for trouble at that hour, so whose fault is it if they find it? I have done a lot more for the burglary problem around Baker's Park than a hundred dumb "watchdogs," believe me.

Gerry-Anne is not only talking to me again, she has invited me to go on a double-date with her. Some guy she met at a party invited her, and he has a friend. They're both from Fawcett Junior High across town, which will be a change. I was nervous, but finally I said yes. We're going to the movies next weekend. My first real date! I am still pretty nervous, to tell the truth.

For New Year's, I have made two solemn vows.

One is that on this date I will not worry about my chest, I will not be self-conscious, even if the guy stares.

The other is, I'll never eat another dog.

Moon Running

Judy Brewer

The weird, half-human creature hunkered under the dark pines at the edge of the clearing, its wolf-like eyes drawn to the descending moon. Still throbbing from the bloodlust, the creature peered out from the shadows as the bright sphere pulled itself free of the clinging, shredded clouds and filled the forest with light. The thing stirred, drawn to its white power. Here was the ultimate deity, Ruler of Night, the all-seeing eye. Even so, the monarch was not perfect. Not yet round. Not quite whole.

The creature whined in frustration. Though the blackness beneath the trees offered concealment, the creature yearned to break free of the shadows and dance in the open moonlight, celebrating the joy of the kill. Then the old torment resurfaced. It had killed and had taken pleasure in the kill. Somehow, that was wrong. Exactly why, the creature didn't know, yet it knew.

One forefoot throbbed. The creature raised the swollen paw-finger, turning it front to back to look at it. One blackened nail had been torn completely off. Gingerly, it licked the wound, tasting its own blood.

Not sure what to do or where to go, it waited in the darkness, squinting at the sky. The moon dropped behind the mountains, and with its passing, the creature shuddered. Something said the change was coming again. *Time to go. Time to return to the jaws of hell.*

Customers at Monty's Truck Stop came big and burly and with appetites to match. They liked breakfast anytime from four a.m. to midnight, coffee strong and black, side orders of bacon, Tabasco on their eggs, and the television on the bar turned up full blast.

One trucker sat at the counter, smothering a double omelet with ketchup. When Sharon walked through the door, he turned with a grin. "Hey, good-lookin'."

"Hey, Ron," Sharon answered, hanging her sweater on a hook. She wasn't in the mood for chatter. Her head felt like a semi had run over it.

Behind the grill, Montana waved a greasy spatula. Sharon didn't say a word, just headed for the time clock.

"Half-hour late, Sharon?" her boss called from behind a cloud of hamburger smoke. "Hustle up. Every trucker in Alberta stopped by this mornin' and the lunch bunch'll be bustin' down the door in a minute. Pull some more burgers from the freezer."

"Right." Sharon punched in as she walked to the freezer in the back room.

"Hurry up," Monty called after her. "Two rigs just pulled up."

"Keep your pants zipped, Montana," Sharon snapped, shivering in the freezer's cold breath. "Let me wash up, will you?" Montana was usually a good-natured guy and didn't deserve that kind of mouth, but she couldn't help it. Since she woke up that morning, she'd felt like hell. Every muscle ached. She'd taken three Tylenol, but it wasn't much better. It didn't matter. She couldn't miss work.

Being a waitress at a truck stop down the long stretch between Edmonton and nowhere wasn't much of a job, but she couldn't complain. It wasn't easy getting work if you were always on the move, and working for Montana was better than some of the dead-end jobs she'd put up with the past two years. Two years. That was as far back, as much of a past as she could remember.

And now the dizzy spells were getting bad again. Four or five days a month, they came and went—disorientation, pain, and then the blackouts. That was what really scared her. Last night, for instance, she couldn't remember a thing after she left Monty's at ten p.m.

Sharon leaned over the sink and splashed water in her face. Monty was yelling at her again through the door. "Coming!" She patted her hair and pasted on a smile before going out to face the customers.

"More pie, Ron?" she asked, refilling coffee for the slump-shouldered, balding giant at the counter, wiping her hands on her apron and pulling the order pad and a pencil from her pocket.

The man picked his teeth with a toothpick. "Yeah, cute buns. One for the road."

She was just turning to cut a wedge of apple pie when a slim, clean-cut man wearing a blue plaid shirt pushed open the door and smiled at her.

"Hey, Doc," Monty greeted from over the grill.

"Hey, Montana," the man returned, focusing his attention on Sharon as he approached the counter. "Hey, Sharon," he added, grinning.

"Doctor Harston." Sharon finished placing the pie in a carry-out box and handed it to the customer. "Ring you up at the cash register, Ron."

"Honey, you can ring me up anytime, anyplace," the trucker wagged his eyebrows.

Sharon snorted. "Shut up, and just pay your bill. Animal."

He howled, going out the door.

"Cut yourself?" the blue-shirted man asked, noticing a Band-Aid on Sharon's fingertip. His eyes glinted. "I can fix that. I am a doctor. C'mere. I'll kiss it better."

She laughed. "Ever hurt yourself and didn't realize you did it 'til later?"

He held up his own finger, bandaged. "Can't say I have. I felt this enough to know it happened, I tell you. Sliced it on a scalpel."

Sharon winced. "Hate it when that happens."

"Hey Doc," Monty said, coming out to the counter. "Whadya make of the wolf killin's we got happenin' round here lately?"

The doctor accepted a cup of coffee from Sharon. He blew on it, taking a long, slow sip before answering. "No one's sure it's a wolf, Montana."

"Hey, it's obvious." Monty rubbed his nose with a forearm. "What else would it be?"

Sharon walked over to take orders from the truckers at the tables, but her ears were tuned to the conversation at the counter.

"Wolverine," the doctor suggested. "Puma. Maybe bear."

"Maybe," Monty argued. "But I say wolf. I got a feelin' deep down. Don't feel safe. Went and got some extra ammo for my .357 magnum yesterday. That thing could come outta nowhere."

The doctor put the cup on the saucer and rubbed his chin. "Now, Montana. I never heard of a wolf attacking a human before, except in the movies. Have you?"

"Yes, I have," Monty insisted, jutting out a whiskered jaw. "There are stories up here. Sam Walking-Far says, way in the backwoods, there's a kind of wolf..."

The doctor chuckled. "Old Sam's stories aren't always gospel truth, y'know, Montana."

"Yeah, well, sometimes these old Indians know more than they get credit for. Sam says his grandpa tells of a wolf that haunted these very parts, about twenty years ago. Came at a man one night when he went to take out the garbage, frothin' at the mouth..."

"The man or the wolf?" The doctor winked at Sharon, returning to the counter.

Monty glared. "The wolf, of course."

"Well, course, rabies is a different story. I'd run from a chipmunk with rabies."

"This wasn't no regular wolf, I tell ya. It was huge. Leaped up and took the man's head clean off with one swipe. In the morning, when he was found by his wife, half of him was *eaten*."

Sharon's eyes widened. Her hand started shaking so much she nearly dropped a cup.

"I won't say it couldn't happen," the doctor said. "But it sounds more like Hollywood hype to me. I wouldn't put much stake in it. From all I've read, it goes against the nature of a wolf to even come near a human, much less kill him, much less *eat* him. Pumas, on the other hand, have been known to take down a man now and then if they're starving and the opportunity presents itself. Bear'll do it just to be ornery."

The doctor smiled oddly, then suddenly leaned forward with a hissed whisper. Sharon, nervously wiping glasses at the sink, started at the sound. "C'mere, Montana," he said, reaching in his shirt pocket. "You, too, Sharon, if you want to see something you'll never forget."

Together, Sharon and Monty bent over the closed fist the doctor held forth. Slowly the fingers opened. It was a claw, a good two inches long. A dried gobbet of flesh clung to its base.

Monty pulled back, gagging. The hair rose on Sharon's neck as she looked on, fascinated. "What is it?" she asked.

"You're so interested in the killings, Monty, well, this was taken from Ben Allred's horse."

Monty's jaw dropped. "The one killed last night?"

The doctor nodded and smiled, satisfied with the reaction. Sharon noticed the white of his teeth. It startled her more than his words.

He went on. "I know the vet who investigated it. He showed it to me this morning and I talked him out of it with a twenty-dollar bill. Vet said it was found stuck between the horse's ribs behind his heart, that is, where his heart *should* have been. There *was* no heart. Pretty grizzly, eh, Sharon? You can see, can't you, Montana, this claw's way too big for a wolf."

For once, Monty was speechless. And green. Without a word, he disappeared into the kitchen. Sharon guessed he'd gone to the toilet to puke. "Why'd you want a thing like that?" she asked, intrigued.

"Souvenir."

Sharon leaned on the counter, order pad in hand. It bothered her the way he watched her. She avoided his eyes.

"Now that you've killed everyone's appetites, what'll you have, Doc?" she asked, over her shoulder, busying herself refilling the coffee pot.

"Please Sharon, call me Alex," he begged, the tone of his voice changing. She recognized a purposeful cordiality to the tone, testing her receptiveness.

"Okay, *Alex*, what'll you have?"

"Depends. What's good today?"

She paused a moment before answering. To be truthful, the smells of the place were getting to her right now—the lifeless slabs of beef and the sweet, sticky smell of ketchup the truckers insisted on smearing over everything—for some reason, they annoyed her.

"Sharon? Did you hear me? What's good?"

"Oh," she startled. How easily distracted she was of late. "Sorry, Alex. Shoulda got more sleep last night. I feel like a helluva grump."

He reached out and brushed her hand with his fingertips. "Then, pretty lady, let me take you away from all of this. Just for a night. Come over to my place. Wine, candlelight—I'm a genius with a grill and I've got two salmon filets in the fridge. What do you say?"

Sharon paused. He'd been after her from nearly the first day she came to town. He was single, she knew, well-off, damned good-looking, popular with the ladies. Even so, she felt no particular attraction to him, or to any other man. She asked herself many times if something was wrong with her. Was she capable of love? Or was there some deep, dark secret in that black, unknown past that held her heart captive?

She stared at him, deciding. He did have a charming smile. He'd want her to spend the night. Hell. Why not? What could it hurt? It'd beat sleeping at the motel.

"I'm closing tonight. Not off 'til ten. That all right?"

"Well, call me a doctor, I'm gonna faint! She said yes!" he laughed.

Then, with a whisper, "I'm very happy, Sharon. Thank you. Eleven, it is. Shall I pick you up here?"

Sharon nodded and turned away, hiding the strange, sudden tinge of resentment behind her eyes. She hated it when she really didn't want to do something, then did it anyway. But when the headaches and dizzy spells came, as they did every month, she often did things she couldn't explain.

Sharon jumped at the honk from Alex's truck. An uneasy feeling had been growing in the pit of her stomach since the sun went down. Not anxiety, as any woman might feel on a first date with a rich, handsome man, more like irrational irritability.

"Montana, I feel like I want to bite something. Or someone," she grumbled, giving the counter a final swipe for the night. "God, either I have hydrophobia or PMS."

"You ask Doc Harston for a shot," Monty snorted. "Right on the backside. He'd love it."

"Think I'll pass. G'night, Montana."

"Hey, watch yourself," Monty called from the kitchen. "That one, he's a hunter."

She stopped short, her hand on the doorknob. "What do you mean?"

"He eats sweet young things like you for breakfast." He winked.

"I can handle him," Sharon said over her shoulder, letting the screen door slam behind her.

In the car, they were silent at first. Both of them knew where the night would end, but neither seemed sure how to begin.

"I collect things," Alex began at last.

"Oh," Sharon responded. "What?"

"Oddities. I like oddities," he said. "I'm always on the lookout for something mysterious."

"Like what?"

"I've got a finger from the Civil War."

"You're kidding."

"Nope. The real thing, vacuum-sealed in plastic. Union soldier. It was sent to his wife. Still had the wedding ring on."

"Claws. Fingers. Not your everyday trinkets, Doc."

"That's just the beginning. I've got one of the bullets that killed

Jesse James and a real scalp taken off a soldier of the seventh cavalry at Little Big Horn."

Sharon was intrigued. "How do you get stuff like that?"

"You have to know the right people," Alex said. "Kind of expensive but it's worth it to me. I admit it; the macabre fascinates me."

Sharon watched him from the corners of her eyes without turning her head, hiding her disgust. "Why?"

He seemed to consider a moment before answering. "I guess it's my profession. I see people die, so naturally, I'm always thinking about it. A guy's eyes roll back in his head and his breath comes out from his lungs like a long sigh, like his soul's saying farewell. And then, he's gone, just like that. One minute, alive. The next, dead and cold."

"You really get off on that kind of stuff?"

He glanced at her, taking his eyes momentarily from the road, then back again. Sharon stared forward, focusing on the beams of the truck's headlights. Trees leaned on both sides of the narrow road, cutting off escape. Darkness closed around them like a trap.

"It's like this, Sharon," Alex said, his voice seeming loud in the empty space between them. "I wonder what it's really like—death, I mean. I think I'd like to know for my own peace of mind. Is it a dreamless sleep, like Shakespeare said, or is there another life to wake up to? Maybe, it's just nothing…" His voice drifted off.

Sharon cocked an eyebrow. "And you think collecting fingers and scalps is going to help you understand death?"

Reaching into his shirt pocket, Alex withdrew the claw he'd shown Sharon at the truckstop. It gleamed darkly in his open palm.

"I don't know," he said, "but when I stare at a thing like this and concentrate, it's like I can almost imagine what it's like."

"It?"

"You know. Taking that last breath; it's like death is here, right here, in my hand. Hey," he laughed nervously, "you probably think I'm demented by now."

He wasn't far off, but at least he wasn't boring.

"I still don't see how you come up with things like that," she said with a grimace. "They'd be pretty hard to find unless you belong to a society of ghouls."

Alex snickered. "You're funny, Sharon. There's an element of luck involved. Being in the right place at the right time."

"You feel lucky tonight?" Sharon asked, her tone suddenly serious.

He turned toward her, smiling. "That's up to you." She stiffened, noticing how white his teeth were in the darkness.

An uncomfortable silence returned, lasting until they arrived at Alex's cabin. To Sharon, walking toward the place on Alex's arm, it looked like something from the cover of *Field and Stream*—your basic A-frame with heavy timber beams, a massive rock chimney and three dark glass front windows reflecting the moon. When Sharon saw that white eye staring back at her as if it were trapped inside the house, the uneasiness she'd felt earlier returned. Her heart quickened. She almost couldn't breathe, feeling trapped inside her body—trapped like the moon—and she *had* to break free.

She stopped abruptly on the walk. "Alex," she said between clenched teeth, straining to maintain control over the madness creeping through her veins. "It's been a hard day, and frankly, I need to unwind. Can we go for a walk or something before dinner?"

"Sure," he said. "There's a path behind the house leading to my own private lake. No one goes there."

"Fine," she said, gripping his arm a little too tightly. Why was it she felt like taking sudden flight? She was no knee-knocking virgin. The idea of being in Alex's bed didn't frighten her, yet, something did, something completely unreasonable—a nameless fear that traveled up and down her spine like an electric current. She could barely control her panic. With all the will she could muster, she stayed on his arm, close to his side, as they walked down the path into the woods.

The forest danced with silver patches of light forking through the black stands of pine. Crickets pulsed a soft rhythm in the background while a warm wind, soft as fur, played through the branches. Temporarily distracted from her fear, Sharon turned her nose into the breeze, drinking in the secret scents of night. With primal delight, her nostrils flared, drawing in every subtle, intricate trace of life.

Alex was babbling on about the stars or something when she first felt the change begin. Her limbs felt tingly, itchy. She shuddered and rubbed her arms.

"Cold?" Alex asked, pulling her close. "Let me warm you up." He stopped, turned her face upward to his and bent to kiss her. The smell of his breath was sweet, unnatural, mannish. It turned her stomach.

Her mind spun away as the moon called. A wild urge she could not deny rose within her, tearing apart the last remaining shreds of self-control. With a cry, she lurched from his arms and ran off down the path into darkness.

"Sharon?" Alex asked, following. "Where are you going? Is this a game? You want me to chase after you?"

"I can't help it, Alex," she called over her shoulder, running with her arms open and free, turning from the path into the trees. Her voice followed behind her in pieces, broken by her panting: "I...just...have...to...run!"

Through the dark forest she raced, in and out of the dappled pools of moonlight, chasing a madness she could not control. Her limbs ached with joy, like the pain of a wild thing prying free of a womb at its birth. She felt reborn, remade for another life. She was changing, she could tell, reclaiming her spirit through a different body—swift, powerful, wild, but not yet whole.

Breaking free at last from all that held her bound, she leaped from shadow into a clearing flooded with moonlight and stopped, trembling with exhilaration. She could hear Alex a long way off, coming after her, cursing, stumbling, heaving for breath. She waited in the shadows, eyeing him as he approached.

He stepped into the light and squinted into the darkness. "Sharon?" he whispered. "Where are you?"

"Here, in the shadows."

"Are you all right? Your voice sounds different."

"I'm wonderful."

"Why did you do that? Come out where I can see you."

"I prefer to stay here if you don't mind," she answered softly. "I'll come in a moment. Right now, I'm enjoying the flavor of night. You're tired, Alex. Sit down and catch your breath."

Silently, with eyes trained on his every move, she watched him collapse on a log. "Aren't *you* tired after all that?" he asked, holding his hand to his chest.

"No," she said truthfully. "I like to run."

She saw him squint his eyes, as if trying to adjust his vision to the darkness to see her. She stood very still.

"You're a strange one, Sharon. From your looks, I'd think you've had a lot of men in your life, yet you ran from me like a scared rabbit. Are you afraid of me?"

"No. Are you afraid of me?"

He laughed. "Should I be?"

"Perhaps."

The silence that followed seemed to make him nervous. He stood up and started toward her. "Why don't we…"

"No, Alex," her tone thwarted him. "I want to talk awhile. Can we just talk awhile? Is that all right?"

"Sure, I guess so," he stood still, rotating his head, "if you want to. What do you want to talk about?"

She waited a moment to answer. Her dark eyes glinted as she looked back at him. "Have you ever felt like you're not yourself, Alex?" Her voice was low, edged with regret. "Have you ever felt like someone else was hiding inside you?"

"What do you mean?" He sounded a bit put off.

"I, I have these dizzy spells," she began, suddenly glad to talk about the thing that so frightened and thrilled her at the same time. "Every once in a while, I blank out. I awake to find myself in strange places, sometimes miles away from where I live, with no explanation of how I got there."

As if perplexed, Alex sat back down on the log. "Well, that's not good. I could give you a check up, if you'll just come here…"

Her teeth shone in an almost-smile. "You just want an excuse to take off my clothes."

He played her game. "Perhaps."

She liked that. It didn't excite her sexually, but for some reason, it was fun to play with him this way, choosing her time.

"You know," he said, "really, Sharon, you should have something like that checked. Periodic amnesia is symptomatic of several things that could be quite serious. Maybe I should book you for an MRI at the hospital over in Edmonton. Are there any other symptoms?"

She settled into a crouch. "Yes. I get these strange feelings. Every four weeks or so."

"Describe them to me."

"All right. My senses become keener. Things like the scents in the air—they become so clear to me, as if I can read them, visualize what made them, a rabbit or a mole or a human."

She saw Alex stiffen. "I gotta tell you that's odd, Sharon. Really odd."

"And my eyes," she went on, "I can see in the dark. Like right now, everything's as clear to me as it is to you in daylight."

"Sharon, maybe we need to head back now…"

"And sometimes, I feel this wild, uncontrollable urge to run like I did tonight, like I could run forever and ever. But what's disturbing, Alex, what's really disturbing is, I get this hunger, a taste in my mouth. It's there now. I want, I need, something sweet, warm, salty..."

"Well, good. Good," Alex clapped his thighs with his hands and stood up. "I'm glad you brought that up. Let's get back to those salmon, shall we?"

"Each time it happens," Sharon went on, rising to her feet with perfectly controlled stealth, "I feel like I'm falling off the edge of the world."

Slowly, she began to circle him, her footsteps silent behind the trees. "It's like falling into a pit. One day, I'm afraid I'll never get back out. I'll just stay there, wherever it is I am."

Alex looked genuinely worried now. He seemed to know she was moving around because he kept turning his face from side to side, following the sound of her voice. His eyes were wide, his skin death-pale in the moonlight. She wondered if he would run for it, but he didn't. Not yet. Maybe he was still more curious than scared.

"I have heard of some forms of psychotic behavior like that," he answered, knotting and unknotting his hands, "where a person feels like there are two people inside, each battling the other to take over. If you're feeling anything like that, Sharon, you ought to see a shrink. Don't take that as an insult. A lot of people..."

"That's just it, Alex. I don't feel like *people* anymore. I feel like a wild thing, a thing that needs to run free, dance in the moonlight, hide in the shadows. A thing that needs to hunt...to feed."

"Sharon," he stepped backward, as if he intended to bolt. "I think you need help."

"No, Alex, you're the one who needs help. But I believe you said there's no one for miles around. No one to come if you call out. No one here but us."

The dark pines loomed over the clearing, and the moon burned above like a cold eye. But for a soft breathing, the forest was completely still. And then the killing began.

Autumn's wind brushed the she-wolf's face. She'd been running for two glorious nights, and now she was almost there, almost home. The scents and sounds of the forest gathered around her.

Everything was in focus, whole once more.

Now that she was herself again, she could remember it all. Her memory was rain-clear and the horror of it stalked her through the night. She could not outrun it. She had been *human*.

There was no explaining it. The sickness had plagued her pack for generations, infecting individuals at random. The others she had known with the disease—the ones who had returned to the pack— were struck again every few years or so. Of those, many were never seen again. Where they went, what happened to them, no one knew. That fear bit at her ankles now. Her time would come again.

The hardest part was being half in, half out, caught in the confusion. Each moon-time, the insanity played its sadistic joke: a promise of freedom from the human form holding her prisoner; the joy of being herself again, almost. Then came the cruel realization that she was still possessed, half wolf, half beast.

In her rage, she killed the loathsome humans and ate their flesh. Dishonor. Humans were lawless, immoral, unclean creatures, yet she had relished their blood. Remembering, bile rose in her throat.

But this time was different. This time, the transformation was complete. Tonight, she ran free, her feet swift, her eyes fire. Tonight she was whole.

She stopped at the top of the next ridge and lifted her voice to the full, perfect moon. From far across the silver-lit valley, an answer came, an invitation to return.

It gave her courage. Perhaps there would be solace in the order of her real world. Perhaps she could forget, until it came again. It would come again and there was nothing she could do.

Terror behind her, terror ahead.

With one last howl, she cried out her anguish then turned, disappearing into the night.

A Model of Transformation

Renée M. Charles

While it's true that the Accalia-Marrok Modeling Agency isn't exactly the biggest or the most famous independent modeling agency in the world, the way in which we pick out prospective girls from that slippery ocean of portfolios sent via priority mail doesn't differ all that much from the manner in which the model agents at Casablanca, Elité, or wherehaveyou choose their girls: no matter how tall or how comely or how finger-down-the-throat slim she may be, if she doesn't have that certain look, forget it. Oh, she might do well enough as a catalogue model or as runway fodder for the up-and-maybe-coming designers who can't afford anyone "known," but if the eyes under that doe-like coating of liner and false lashes don't have that in-the-soul fire, the glimmer of something more, well, let's just say that *Fashion TV* won't be doing a profile anytime soon.

Whenever I do see a girl with that look, I literally have to have her, whether she's all that eager to become a model or not. Like Faoitiarna Bleidd. Tiarna, now, to all of her wannabe followers.

Before there was ever a Tiarna, there was a shy, reticent Faoitiarna, with timid, downcast eyes and the unruly pelt of silvery-blond hair, standing on that little bridge across the street from the Guthrie Theater in the Twin Cities (which one of those twin burgs I can never quite recall). The grounds beyond the theater/gallery were beautiful; park-like, yet tame enough to suit this city gal. Not quite as expansive as Central Park, but the little bridge was quaint, and the girl who stood bundled in an ill-fitting Minnesota Timberwolves jacket against the slight spring chill was utterly stunning.

The early afternoon sunlight caught the natural silver highlights in her simply pushed-back mane, even as it cast delicate bluish-pale shadows under her high cheekbones. Her jeans-clad legs were exquisitely long and lean, just firm enough in the calf to fill out those narrow tubes of denim tautly yet elegantly. Her bulky jacket-clad arms were crossed high on her chest, yet didn't stick out all that far; she couldn't have been anything more than a barely filled B-cup. My heart began lopping under my own Wonderbra-augmented B-cup as I walked closer to her, barely able to breathe for fear of some-how spooking this silvery vision—losing her before I'd had the chance to make my pitch. When she finally noticed me, she only quivered in place for a moment, looking as if she wished to flee, but didn't. She did, however, lower her eyelids so that I could see only a glimmering sliver of a pale green-gray eye through the feathery sweep of dark-brown lashes. Those half-closed eyes held that *look*....

"Has anyone ever told you that you should be a model?" She shook her head no. "My name is Lewanna Velvel. I'm an agent with the Accalia-Marrok Agency..." Before I could stop myself, I blurt-ed out, "You must wake up looking drop-dead gorgeous. I can't imagine you looking any other way." Only after the words were uttered did I realize how completely ingenuous I sounded. And that she didn't seem to mind at all.

"My name is Faoitiarna Bleidd, and in case you're wondering, it's Irish and Welsh, though I'm neither. Still, I find it suits me. Very well."

"Faoitiarna Bleidd. Do you mind if I call you Tiarna?"

I took Tiarna to a new designer. Fridolph was young, gay, and eager to get a leg up in the business. As she ran those elegantly long, shiny-tipped fingers across his hangered garments, lightly touching the shoulders of each piece, I noticed that he was swallowing con-vulsively. I'd personally seen Fridolph mingling with a dressing room full of half-naked models without so much as casting a lin-gering glance at a one of them. Fridolph was a boy's boy, but there was something about my newest discovery that even he couldn't ignore. "Such a scent," he warbled.

"Do you think she'll make it on the runways?"

"She'll eat 'em alive...and make everyone else wish they were feasting on her."

She appeared in the hallway bearing a floating wisp of a bias-cut red chiffon over raw silk that revealed her thin yet well-formed bare arms and her reed-like neck. It was the reflection of her dress that gave her eyes a special look, a different caste: an inhuman, chilling glare that set off her incisors.

Beside me, Fridolph unconsciously began to cross himself, muttering something I couldn't quite understand. "I don't know if these shoes go with this dress," she said apologetically as she looked down at the pair of black leather lace-ups.

"Not to worry. Fridolph, you have a box of shoes that your models wear, don't you?" I burbled cheerfully as I rooted about the cardboard box of shoes he kept on hand. I found a pair of red spikes and handed them over to Tiarna. "Doesn't matter if they don't fit. You'll have to get used to wearing shoes that don't fit at every runway show..."

"The fit's no problem," she replied with a serrated smile....

After we bid a rushed adieu to Fridolph (who finally composed himself enough to whisper in my ear as I air-kissed his cheek, "Keep this one on a short leash, dearheart") there was just enough time to make it to the airport. I lost sight of Tiarna amid the pressing, bustling rush of boarding passengers, but I knew it wasn't merely my imagination when I could still smell her intense, volatile cologne despite the fact that she was sitting in another section of the plane. Even an hour after take-off, all I had to do was inhale deeply and it was as if she was close by me again.

Years ago, I read somewhere that odor molecules, once inhaled, remain in one's lungs and become a part of the person's body. If that was truly so, Tiarna had long since become as one with me. From the first moment I came close enough to breathe in her unique bouquet, she and I had begun to merge.

Midway through the flight, lulled by the almost imperceptible vibration of the cabin and the "lite instrumentals" channel playing over my earphones, I began to doze. Although I can't recall all of my dream, I remember a dazzling gray-green-yellow-eyed creature with flesh both silvery and nappy soft. I could feel the sensation of running, running, not just on two legs.... "Lewanna...Lew-wa-nnaaa..."

The voice was so close to my ear that at first it melded with my dream, the syllables of my name uttered in time with the rhythmic, loping motions of my four legs. Then the plane hit an air-bump, a small one, but enough to gently rock the cabin, enough to wake me, even as that teasing voice continued to drawl, "Lew-wa-nnaaa..."

Turning my head in the direction of the voice, I found myself almost cheek-to-cheek and lip-to-lip with Tiarna who was sitting in the chair that had been formerly occupied by a chubby grandmother from Edina who was on her way to her grandson's graduation from Syracuse. Before I could ask where Grandma had gone, my latest would-be supermodel informed me that she'd met my seatmate just outside the restrooms. "She was so curious about the seating in first class, and since I realized that her empty seat in business was next to you..."

"I just had the weirdest dream. You and I...we...we were running side by side, only on all fours, like some sort of animals." It was then that Tiarna crossed her bare legs so that her right calf and spike-heeled foot were resting against my own legs, and in the slanting light from the overhead fixture, I noticed that Tiarna's legs were covered with a fine coating of silvery hair, which clung tightly to the sinuous curves and hollows of each achingly long limb. As I glanced at her arms resting in her red-draped lap, I saw that they, too, had that same protecting layer of almost invisible silver-blond hair, which even covered the spaces between her knuckles, all the way down to each elongated oval of nail.

"What sort of animals?" she asked in a teasing, deep-in-the-throat purr while raking her fingers through her shaggy mane of luxurious, rippling hair. I angled my head close to the nape of her neck and whispered, "When we get to New York, after we get to the hotel, we must talk..."

All she did was nod and smile her smile in reply.

She'd been silent but watchful during the taxi ride to the hotel, but once we were checked in and the bellboy had left with tip in hand, she kicked off her shiny, red, spiked heels and padded barefoot over to the huge window that faced the lush greenness of the park below. She stood there, mouth slightly open, hands pressed palms outward against the sun-warmed glass. Her chest heaved with deep, shuddering inhalations of the stuffy hotel room air. I watched her for a few seconds, then asked, "Why did you say your name suited you, back there in Minnesota?" I inhaled deeply of her perfume and moved slowly behind her until I could just barely feel the radiant warmth of her jutting shoulders and partly exposed back.

"It suits me because it describes me. Not like my old names."

I gently ran one forefinger along her back until I could no longer feel her spine, but instead felt the slight outward curve of her but-tocks. "And just how old are you?"

There was a pause as she inclined her head toward the glass, her silvery solidity ghosted by her translucent reflection.

"Young enough to feel strong, yet.... Everything around me has changed. People respond differently to me. Just as I..." She let her voice trail off even as she arched her backside against my barely hov-ering hand so that I could rest my palm against the spot where her tail might have been.

"Doesn't your name mean 'moon' in Hebrew?" she asked.

"I never really thought about it, but it is a Hebrew name," I said, lifting my hand from her back. "I've studied names," she said, "His name was Raoul. Raoul Hrollief. I knew that Raoul meant 'wolf' in French, but 'Hrollief'? It was only after we'd been together, close enough for him to cover my breasts and neck with those little love-nips of his, that he told me it was old Norse for 'wolf.' Raoul wasn't a killer. None of our kind really are, just as wolves aren't ferocious predators. They're shy creatures, unless challenged."

"You can't be shy if I sign you with my agency," I said slowly as I reached over to draw the curtains. "You'll have people staring at you, touching you, touching your hair, applying your makeup. And of course, you won't be able to work whenever there's a full moon..."

"Isn't that what schedules are for?" she asked. Even as the insanity of the situation invaded my mind ("I'm sorry, but my client can't work the week of a full moon") I could see that this was the solution. I could easily juggle assignments for her to avoid those days when she'd be covered with more than the silvery down, when her scissor-ing gait turned to a carefree lope. I longed to witness that lycanthropic transformation, albeit in the privacy of my own apartment where I could cast aside the draperies and allow the moonlight to stream in unimpeded, to caress and transfigure her lithe, silken body....

While all those plans ran through my mind, Tiarna grasped the hem of her bias-cut skirt and asked me, "Will I have to undress in front of rooms full of people?" before she shucked off the filmy dress in a fluid, rippling motion of supple musculature and gracefulness, tossing the silk and chiffon onto the bed behind her.

Even in the diffuse light that filled the room, I could see that her entire torso was covered with a shimmering silver down, which thick-ened in a straight line down her concave belly and spread luxuriously across her thickly covered, slightly swollen mons before spreading in a lighter shadowing of curling hair across the inner portions of her thighs. She was still the most beautiful woman I'd ever beheld. I ran my hands lightly over Tiarna's small, jutting breasts and slid them palms-down across her narrow, taut waistline and barely flared hips before pausing at the soft swell of her behind. "Rooms and rooms full of people...girls, guys, whatever. There's just one little problem..."

Tiarna reached behind her and placed her long, tapering hands over mine, pressing my palms tighter against her flesh. "A little cosmetic work, perhaps?"

While I initially considered taking Tiarna down to one of those open-all-hours beauty barber shops, I soon realized it would be difficult to explain all that hair, and in so many places on her body, so I decided to begin the process in the privacy of our room.

Once we were together in the bathroom with the door closed behind us, and Tiarna's bare, radiant body reflected in the many mirrors and shiny tiled surfaces, I couldn't resist doffing my own clothes and joining her in the large, glass-walled shower stall. When wet, the hair on her head and body took on an oleographic, rainbow sheen, the individual hair parting against her flesh to form hundreds of runnelling patterns of meandering water droplets. When the pummeling spray hit her, a fine mist of steam rose from her already warm flesh, enveloping her in a cloud-like haze. When our water-slicked skin met breast to breast and thigh to thigh, I found myself barely able to stand from the heady feeling of excitement and anticipation. Tiarna adjusted the nozzle of the showerhead, she unwrapped the small bar of motel soap and began to run the rectangle of creamy white against my flesh, leaving a bubbling trail of foam along each breast, then down my belly, and finally over and around my throbbing mons, not stopping until the thatch of dark curls was stiff with lather. Only then did she begin to massage my body with those long, sinuous fingers, their heat almost searing my wet, trembling flesh.

When she reached my foaming, aching labia, Tiarna probed my slippery depths with her fingers before kneeling down amid the pummeling spray of woman droplets. Using her long, keenly pointed tongue on my lower belly, she wiggled it deep within the cleft to the core of my being, lightly raking my tender flesh with those sensuously elongated incisors...and when I came, it was all I could do to keep hold of the safety bar behind me as I felt myself consumed by one shuddering wave of orgasm after another.

As the last ripple of orgasm coursed through me, I looked down at my heaving, dripping body and realized that, despite the dental teasing Tiarna had inflicted on my tender skin, she hadn't pierced my flesh. She alone was still afflicted with the "curse" of the *loups-garoux*.

When she got up off her knees and stood in all her dripping, steaming glory before me, I think she saw the glint of disappointment in my eyes. She quit the shower stall and toweled herself off.

She began slathering her arms, legs and torso with the harsh-smelling hair removal lotion. While the odor of the creme was disturbingly piquant, her own natural, intense bouquet soon masked it.

Knowing that I wouldn't be able to stop myself from massaging the creme into her skin, I instead busied myself with the rest of my shower, even as I stole peeks at her through the cloudy glass. Once the allotted time had passed and Tiarna re-entered the shower stall, she didn't need to ask me to use the detachable shower wand to wash away the last vestiges of hair remover.

The difference in her skin was remarkable. What was once downy and softly metallic was now smooth and shiny, an expanse of slippery clean skin, save for the tangle of pale curls covering her mons and, of course, the thick thatch on her scalp.

Within minutes, we were out of the shower stall and bundled in thick motel robes and towels anticipating our first night together. Later, over bottles of Nördick Wolf Light beer brought up by room service, and plates of caviar and sliced cheeses, she and I planned the rest of our stay in the city: While I attended my appointed meetings and showings, she would soak up as much about the business as possible, and between my scheduled duties for the agency, we'd visit hairdressers, clothing stores, shoe stores, and a promising new makeup artist whose career I'd been following closely—plus fit in as much shower time as possible.

By the time Tiarna and I settled into our first-class seats on the plane to Toronto a few days later, we were both different people; for my part, I'd never been so completely, uninhibitedly satisfied by anyone, anywhere—a state of bliss that clearly showed on my face and in the small, secret smile I saw whenever I happened to notice my reflection in a passing window. As for Tiarna, I don't know whether it was the wardrobe of Richard Tyler leathers, Miu Miu vinyls, tight Carolina Herrera suits; the sessions under the sun-lamp; or her hair and makeup make-over, but just as sure as every Valentino show features a red dress and something in an animal print, I knew that, signed to an agency or not, Tiarna had arrived.

Needless to say, Rafe Marrok and Lunetta Accalia were impressed with a capital *I*. Rafe personally accompanied her during her initial portfolio shoot, then hand-delivered the results to the editors of *Vogue, Cosmopolitan, Vanity Fair* and whatever other magazine he could squeeze in during his next trip to the Big Apple. Meanwhile, Lunetta convinced the organizers of the next Sonia Rykel, Victor Alfaro, Todd Oldham and Oscar de la Renta shows to just take a look at her, knowing full well that one look alone would be enough.

The down-side to Tiarna's rapid rise to the top was that she was often—far too often—away from my side, from my entire body. I missed the sly, taunting shine of her bright eyes, the sere heat of their gaze on my own flesh. Despite her hectic schedule during those first two weeks of her career, Tiarna and I still managed to spend a couple of evenings together on the roiling warmth of my water bed, still moist from the shower, with our flesh pressed tight-ly together. On the second evening, I noticed her skin was slightly less smooth than usual.

"We'll need to schedule in a session with the removal creme or you'll need to visit the waxing salon," I teased. Tiarna was too dis-tracted to notice the playfulness of my tone, for she shook her head of mousse-sculpted hair and said, "No time. I'm off for Paris tomor-row, for the Leger show..."

"The Leger show isn't until next week. You can't work then, don't you remember?"

"Rafe was quite firm about it. This is a major, major show, and he's certain it will 'make' me as a supermodel," she insisted. I reached over and pulled her head up by the thick thatch of bangs above her forehead, then angled her face toward our open window, through which a fat segment of the three-quarters full, bone-white moon was visible through a wispy scud of clouds.

"How big do you think the moon will be by the time Leger's show arrives? Remember, all we did was remove the fuzz from your body. I don't recall changing anything else about you."

Wiggling out from under my grasp, she flipped over onto her

side, letting her breasts sag slightly on top of each other as she reached over to cup my own breasts in her long, hot hands, then murmured, "Rafe said the show would be in the afternoon and over in plenty of time for me to get a decent night's rest. Perhaps you might be able to wrangle some free time around then, to watch me during the show, and then afterward?"

The sensation of her warm, moist palms caressing my nipples and flattening my breasts against my ribcage was so soothing, so luxurious, all I could do was nod my assent to her suggestion before letting my own hands glide between her loosely closed thighs....

Rafe wasn't terribly happy about me asking for my vacation during the weekend of the Leger show, but he eventually relented. When I got to the place where the show was to be held, I learned that either Rafe had lied, or Tiarna had gotten Paris time mixed up with Toronto time, for the show wasn't to start until early evening and would continue well into the night.

Right in time for the rising moon.

I rushed backstage. At first, I couldn't see Tiarna, but I eventually caught her warm, musky scent and followed her olfactory trail to a distant dressing table where a hairdresser I knew was trying to tame her mane of thickly layered hair into a semblance of sleek, skull-hugging order. Just as I arrived, I noticed that with each tug of the comb through her hair, Tiarna was making little snarling motions with her lips and teeth.

"Half hour to show time. Everybody out who should be out," came a shout from somewhere in that writhing mass of models, makeup and hair people. As I squeezed through the crowd toward the exit, I took one last look at Tiarna and prayed that it was only a trick of the caged makeup lights that made her skin look so luminous and softly shining.

It took some shoving and more than a little calling in favors, but I managed to wrangle a second-row seat during that open-air show. As luck would have it, Tiarna was one of the first women down the catwalk that evening. It wasn't hard for me to make out the unmistakable shimmer of downy hair on her long, exposed arms and pushed-up-from-below breasts. She was wearing stockings, but under the artificial sheen of the sheer fabric, the subtle arabesque of flattened hairs was easily discernible. And the look on her face! Even though her makeup was thick, almost matte, it didn't hide the atavistic glimmer in her eyes as she stalked down that runway, mouth quivering, sometimes pouting, sometimes a near-snarling smear of artfully painted, bright red. And despite the thick dusting of pale powder on her cheeks, I could see the unearthly flush of suffused blood just beneath the surface of her skin.

As she turned on her heel and began to all but lope down the runway back to the dressing area, I silently prayed that she'd twist an ankle in those high heels, or fall down in a Naomi Campbell-style tumble. But I didn't think the god who looks after werewolves was listening that evening. She merely disappeared behind the curtains, while girl after girl came slinking out on the catwalk, shimmying under those tighter-than-skin dresses. Again I prayed that she'd have the sense to go hide herself now that the glare of the full moon was painting the audience and the runway a stark, lunar white. But Tiarna was Tiarna, sometimes shy, but really quite bold, especially when she had that look in her lupine eyes....

It was a full ten minutes before she appeared through those curtains again, more than ample time for the moon to rise high enough in the sky to shine squarely on the runway itself. While she may have looked normal enough not to attract too much attention backstage, wiggling from one skin-hugging dress to a luminous white Hervé with dozens of crisscrossing, body-defining bands, she only made it halfway down the runway before the limits of Hervé's latest creation were put to the most outré test of all:

Hair by hair, over every exposed inch of her body, Tiarna began first to shimmer, then to stumble slightly. Her head hung down, and her long arms slowly and sensuously began to elongate until her knuckles brushed the runway. The audience sucked in its breath as though one, and it was possible to make out the tiny, chitinous sounds of her joints popping and her cartilage stretching under the steadily changing flesh. Her face grew leaner, more distinctly wolfen, and her slicked-down hair began to release from its gooey bonds, framing her swiftly changing features with a mane of thick, shaggy softness, which simultaneously softened and highlighted her face.

While there was the occasional horrified shout of *"loup-garou"* from the audience, some tipping over their folding chairs to escape the scene of Tiarna's metamorphosis, many more people began to cheer, applauding my protégé's unexpected performance.

Hervé was ecstatic. And the press...well, considering that she didn't bite or kill anyone, the press immediately dubbed her the "Transformer of Supermodels." Oh, true, she got some additional press in the tabloids, but her bookings skyrocketed, especially on the nights of the full moon.

That night in Paris, partly in anger, partly in lust, Tiarna covered my aching breasts and arched neck with tiny, stinging love bites deep enough to draw—and mingle—our blood, just as her intense scent had mingled with the very fibers of my lungs.

And when the dark shadow of hair began to cover my body, enveloping me, I was able to witness the transformation in the floor-to-ceiling mirrors in my hotel suite, even as Tiarna began her own transformation from wolf to woman.

Luckily, she still felt up to taking a midnight run with me, and as we loped along the moonlit back street, her footfalls changed to the soft thud of paws along the cobbles, our fur rippling in the night breeze as we ran, shoulder to shoulder, hip to hip, lolling tongues flapping in the cool air, running through the city of love.

While we haven't always been able to synchronize our schedules, we did take the time to rent a cabin in the Northwest Territories, where we could run and play in the majestic silence of the near-primal forest, far from the glare of the runway lights and the piped-in music. But even in the clear, cool woods, I can still see that special glow in Tiarna's eyes, the look that tells me that a part of her will always remain in the hot glare of the moon-bright arc lights and the wind-rushing roar of the applauding audiences.

Werewolf or not, Tiarna's still a true supermodel at heart....

The Final Truth

Steve Eller

Justin clicked his laptop computer closed and set it beside him on the crude wooden bench. He rubbed his eyes; they throbbed from staring too long at the screen in the dim light of dusk. He squinted and looked out across the lake. The sun was setting, a ball of orange fire melting slowly into the gentle waves. Each tiny ripple of dark water carried a sliver of brilliant orange back toward the shore. The glowing shards vanished as the water touched the stony bank.

Justin watched the sun sink until only a glowing halo remained above the darkened surface of the water. He rose and stretched, then headed back toward the cabin. Halfway down the gravel path, he realized he'd forgotten his portable computer.

"If only I could forget it for good," he thought.

Leaves crunched under his feet as he walked back to the bench. He lifted the laptop and tucked it into the crook of his arm. The computer was his solitary link to civilization. After a few years without a vacation, he was more than ready to take his coworkers advice and spend time alone in the mountains. But he wasn't ready to sever his last link just yet.

He listened to the sounds of the forest as he walked toward the cabin: the rustle of leaves in the breeze, the squeaks and rasps of unseen insects, the squawking birds. They were so different from the sounds he was used to: buzzing cellular phones, screeching modems and the steady click of shoes against concrete sidewalks. He felt strange and out of place surrounded by so much nature. It had been years since he'd seen a tree that wasn't in a clay pot in some tiled lobby.

Justin froze as he heard a new sound. It was low and heavy, a rumbling like the hum from a powerful engine. It reminded him of a giant bellows he had seen in one of his father's factories. An even rush of air, in and out, like deep breathing.

His nerves tingling like live wires beneath his skin, Justin forced his leaden feet to move another step. His heart was hammering and his breath became shallow, slicing in his throat. He tried to convince himself that it was nothing, just the irrational fear of a city boy alone in the woods. But his body was telling him something else, and it was bad news. His instincts somehow seemed to know what his mind failed to comprehend.

Justin took a few more dragging steps toward the cabin. He could see the outline of the building in the darkness. One of the tiny front windows glowed, lit by an electric light shaped like an oil lamp. The cabin he'd rented had electricity and running water, even a data jack for his modem. He wanted to rough it, but modern style.

The sound of the breathing paced him as he walked slowly down the path. The front steps were only a few feet away and he tried to keep his stride even, in spite of his intense desire to sprint the rest of the way.

As he started up the steps, Justin got the eerie feeling that he was being watched. A creature born and raised in the city, he asked himself for the hundredth time what he was doing out in the boonies alone. Despite his need to get away from work for a while, he wished he was back home in his apartment, eight stories off the ground and behind layers of security, safe from the countless dangers of the real world.

He raised his hand slowly as he stepped across the porch. The knob was inches away from his fingertips. He noticed his hand was shaking. He heard the strange sound close behind him, felt the imaginary eyes burning the skin along the back of his neck. Sweat trickled down his back. His fingers closed on the metal knob and he turned it.

So close now, he thought. *Another second or two and it'll be over.*

Justin pushed the door open a crack, just wide enough to knife his shoulder in. He slid one foot into the opening and began to pivot into the cabin.

A heartbeat later something hit him—something huge and warm and powerful. His hands and face struck the wooden door as he tumbled inside. The breath spewed from his lungs as his chest struck the floor of the cabin. He heard his PC clatter down and slide away.

A weight landed on his back, crushing and smothering him. Tears welled up in his eyes and he saw the shadowy room through a shimmering curtain. He heard the gasping sound he made as he tried to refill his burning lungs with air. His fingers scrabbled at the floorboards, trying to find a grip.

A moment later, the weight was gone. Heart pounding, he sprang up and scurried into a corner, drawing himself into a tight ball. Hot blood surged through him, heating his face and making him light-headed. His mind whirled with images of danger and death, his body shaking with fear. He looked around for any weapons to be found. There weren't any.

Cool air gradually drifted back into his lungs. Slowly, his blurred vision began to clear. He scanned the room searching for his attacker. The air he swallowed carried a scent: heavy and fleshy, but at the same time, musty and earthy. His body seemed once again to know more than his mind. His tendons tightened as though there were something here to be afraid of, but his mind—his civilized mind—didn't recognize it.

He listened for the deep bellows sound. It was coming from a darkened corner, slowly and evenly. The cabin was dark, lit only by pale moonlight streaming in through the windows. He stared down at the floor and saw glittering slivers of glass. The lamp must have been shattered during the attack.

His eyes slowly adjusted to the darkness, and he gazed into the shadowed corner again. He saw a hazy outline of something large, dark, and hunched. He felt an icy spike in his chest as two brilliant green lights began to shine. He threw his hands to his mouth, as if to catch the heart that threatened to leap out of his throat.

Eyes, he thought. *My God, they're eyes.*

Within the darkness, the darker shape moved. It flowed out toward him like a liquid shadow. It was eerily silent except for the even rasp of its breathing. A pallid sheen traced over its form as it stepped into a crude square of moonlight on the floor.

Even city boy Justin could identify the creature. It was a wolf. It came forward, head lowered, wiry hair bristling over the rippling muscles of its massive shoulders and neck.

Justin felt his blood chill to ice water. He began to shiver, drawing himself into a tighter ball. His mind spun out of control. He wondered again why he had ever left the city. He wondered why he wasn't dead already. He closed his eyes, remembering that it always made the bad thing go away when he was a kid. When he forced himself to look again, it was still there. The animal had stopped and was waiting in a half-crouched position, prepared to spring. He shivered at the thought of its teeth touching him, but the creature stayed still. Long minutes passed. The huge, shaggy head was tilted slightly, as though the burning green eyes were studying him.

Perhaps it was only a trick of the light or his runaway imagination, but Justin thought he saw subtle changes in the huge, silver-gray wolf. Its thick coat seemed to be lightening, thinning. Its outline quivered in the darkness, as though its shape were changing. Justin lowered his face into his hands and rubbed his throbbing eyeballs with his thumbs. Needles of pain lanced back into his head. He took a deep breath and looked up.

He gasped, losing his breath in a rush of vertigo. The wolf was gone; a woman crouched in its place. Reality pitched violently in his mind and he wondered if he had gone insane from pure fright. She stood. Her pale skin was streaked with dirt and laced with a tapestry of scratches. Long, dark hair hung down over her bare shoulders. Justin gazed up into her face. Behind tangles of stray hair, the wolf's green eyes still blazed. He went numb, unable to move. He commanded his body to get up and run, but the tangle of meat and bone refused to stir.

The woman came closer, her bare feet scraping lightly over the floorboards. She dropped to one knee in front of him, reaching out. Justin turned his face away, but her warm hand closed on his chin and wrenched his head back around. The woman was smaller than he, but the strength in her grip was chilling. Her nails were sharp, scraping against his skin. A powerful scent drifted up from her. Of flesh and earth. And sex.

Justin almost laughed in spite of the fear swirling in his belly. He recalled reading in a health magazine that men think of sex every thirty seconds, but this was ridiculous. He had been attacked by a wolf that had somehow become a woman, and he was thinking about sex. But the smell of her was strong, nearly overpowering. It touched something primal in his brain, and his body started to respond.

In a motion too quick for him to see, the woman released his face and grabbed his shirt. She threw him down and dragged him across the floor. He felt like a child in the grasp of an adult: helpless. He knew there was no way to resist as the woman pressed his shoulders to the wooden floor and climbed onto his chest.

He knew he should be deathly afraid. He knew he should fight, but the only thought in his head was that his clothes were too tight, constricting him, standing in the way of his intense desire for sex. He tried to raise his hands and touch her smooth flesh, but she slapped them back down. His arms stung as they struck the floor.

The woman lowered a hand to his chest and shredded his shirt, her fingernails scratching his skin. He found the pain oddly arousing. She slid down his legs, taking his tattered trousers with her.

Her skin burned like liquid fire as she slid over him. He heard a sound like a low growl coming from her throat. He stared up into the brilliant green eyes as she lowered herself onto him. His nerves overloaded—the touch of her fiery flesh, the nails raking his sides. The sensation was too intense—hot, frightening and wild.

An instant later he clenched his teeth and exploded into her. He watched her moist lips rise into what he thought was a smile. She showed her long teeth instead. Justin realized that the danger had only just begun.

Justin gave up on trying to keep his hands clean. The water in the bucket beside him on the floor was already stained a brilliant crimson. His hands came out almost as red as they went in.

He draped another towel over her leg. He had never seen so much blood in his life. His old life. Back then blood was a sure sign of a paper cut. But things had changed for him. He had never dreamed of the surge of power that came from eating raw, steaming flesh. Or from killing your meat with your bare hands. This was real life, the way his life was now. Not wrapping himself inside itchy clothes and surrounding himself with weak people who cower at the sight of pain. Truly living was feeling the struggling muscle between his hands, fighting for its tiny life, and knowing that the life taken would be used to strengthen his own. The woman had taught him so much, told him so many things. Except her name. He wished she would tell him her name.

She screamed again. He held tightly to her ankles, trying to keep her from thrashing across the floor. He had placed a large chunk of wood in each of her hands and one into her mouth. A pile of wood chips grew beside her on the floor. Suddenly she relaxed, moaning softly.

As he stared at the swollen, bloody flesh between her thighs, he thought again how much his life had changed in the last year. At first it had been reduced to a simple cycle of pain and pleasure. Pain when he tried to escape or when he felt weak. Pleasure as she mounted him each night. His fear had gradually died away in the wake of realization. She didn't mean to kill him, only to keep him. The reason she needed him was not for blood, but for birthing. He had figured at first that it was all some sexual domination fetish, but it went on for far too long and was performed too regularly. He realized that she needed to bear a child and that for some reason she had chosen him. Why was still a mystery. The woman rarely spoke and when she did speak, it was to teach or to scold. To tell him about nature. About needs. About life.

It was through her that he had learned the falseness of his human life, of the meaningless layers with which people enshrouded themselves. Laws and timetables, religion and society. He saw through it all now, to the flesh beneath it all, to the reality of blood and life and change and death. It is an endless cycle, and now he was a part of it. Not buying his meat wrapped in plastic and displayed under a fluorescent light, but taking it. Feeling the heat of the muscle that feeds life, feeling it as urgently as he felt his own need.

She allowed him only glimpses of his former self, such as the use of his computer when it became necessary to transfer more funds to keep up the payments on the cabin. And now here he was, face to face with the most primal of nature's forces. Childbirth. *His* child. The child of the werewolf who had taught him the reality of life. He knew what she was, although neither of them had ever spoken the word. He had seen her change, watched her take down her prey. He was only able to follow behind, to catch the smallest of creatures, and only those he outsmarted. She allowed him only the use of his body. She had destroyed a trap he had designed, then punished him with her claws and teeth.

It wasn't long before her body began to change. Her belly and breasts swelled and he knew she was with child. She had continued to hunt up until just a few days before, when she began to make an elaborate nest of blankets on the floor. Then it was time for him to care for her.

Justin tried to remember exactly when his fear had turned to intimacy. As he shed his civilized self, he came to love his new life and the stark beauty of the creature with whom he shared the cabin. The incredible secrets of nature had never really been secrets at all. Just forgotten things.

The woman screamed again. Justin saw a smear of bloody hair

appear between her legs. His heart leapt. He knew it was time. He positioned himself between her raised knees, holding a clean towel to catch the emerging child. The skin of his neck itched, sensing the taut strength in the legs around him. He knew they could crush him in an instant if she chose to close them. He also knew that her heart was strong and that she would endure the pain without moving.

He heard one of the wooden sticks she held in her hand shatter as the infant's head popped out. The tiny face was perfect, glistening red and black. He wasn't surprised at the thick tufts of hair on its head and face. He held the towel gently under the tiny skull to keep it from striking the floor. Already the little face was moving, the tiny jaws trying to open. The eyes were closed, quivering. Justin smiled at the length of the nose, almost like a snout.

The woman's high-pitched scream rattled his skull. The baby fell into his hands in a torrent of blood and dark fluid. He bundled it close against his bare chest, amazed at the heat radiating from the tiny thing. It mewled softly as he placed his cheek against the baby's face. Laying the afterbirth across the child's legs, he crawled on his knees to the woman's side and gave the infant to her. She unwrapped the wet towel and flung it away. She placed the baby across her heaving chest, between her sweat-streaked breasts. Justin felt a lump growing in his throat as he watched. Tears welled in his eyes and began to trickle down his face. He didn't know if he would be punished for such a show of emotion, but he didn't care. It was worth it.

He saw the woman's arm come to rest across the child's back. He thought she intended to hug the child, but to his horror, she extended a fingernail and jabbed its tender skin. Justin moved to stop her, but she kicked him and sent him tumbling across the floor. He raised his eyes and saw her jab the child again and again. A tiny bead of brilliant blood trickled down its legs. A moment later it began to scream and cry and Justin sighed. He realized the woman only meant to clear its tiny throat. He came across the floor and lay beside her. She allowed him to touch the child. He stroked its slick head and arm. He saw that it was a little girl.

The woman raised onto one shoulder and turned away from him, as though shielding the child. He saw dark blood squirt as she severed the cord. A moment later he heard a slow, rasping sound. He closed his eyes and pictured her long tongue working lovingly over the child, licking it clean. He smiled.

Justin woke. He heard a constant wailing and shot straight up from his bundled blankets. His first thought was that something was wrong with the child. He searched frantically around the room, his heart racing. Then he saw them, mother and child together, sitting on the windowsill. The child was trembling and thrashing as the woman tried to calm it, whispering into her ear. He smiled. Soft morning light gleamed around them. The sight warmed his heart. She turned her eyes toward him and stood, cradling the month-old child in her arms.

The woman fell to her knees beside him, holding the agitated child tightly to her chest. Justin reached out, but she held the child back, slowly shaking her head.

"It's time," she said.

Justin was confused, unsure of what she meant.

"Time for what?" It was time to rise, time to eat, but her tone was nearly reverent, like this was a special day. His body tingled with anticipation. He had already learned so many secrets. He knew he was about to witness one more.

The look in the woman's eyes was unknowable. Justin realized that although he had come a long way in shedding his unnatural life, he still had much to learn. Things that glimmered with a dire certainty in the woman's gaze.

"You asked me once to make you like me," the woman said. "Now I will tell you why I did not. Because I cannot. It is not passed that way. Only through the blood. But there are no males. Perhaps there were, once, but not anymore. This is how we survive, mother to daughter."

Justin shook his head, trying to clear his thoughts. These were more words than she had spoken to him since the day she first took him. He tried to make sense out of what she was saying. There was something here, something about nature. Something vital.

"Maybe the males tried to fight," she continued. "Maybe they fell beneath the swelling tide of the human race, smothered by the meat that should have been food. Perhaps the females killed them. I don't know, but there are none left. No more are born. But instinct— nature—burns in me. I cannot let it end with me. My mother taught me, and now I pass it along."

His nerves began to crackle beneath his skin, just as they had on that first night. He had long ago ceased fearing her other than the pain of her punishment, but the fear of death grew in him again. Something was wrong. His new, natural self sensed it as surely as he sensed the nearness of prey.

"Now it is her time to become what she is." She held the screaming child away from her, dropping it to the blankets. "Her hunger for milk alone has ended."

Justin tried to get to his feet, but the woman grasped him and held him down. She glared at him. Her green eyes were bottomless. He searched them for an emotion that he recognized: regret, pity, mercy, or even the lack of it. But he saw nothing. Nothing except for desire. And need. That was nature. She was still teaching him, teaching him by doing what must be done.

He heard it before he felt it. A swift, slashing sound like a blade slicing through the air. A heartbeat later his throat began to throb and sting. He felt the warm blood trickling onto his chest. It bubbled up and over his lips, into his mouth. He tried to crawl away, but his limbs felt weak and cold. Numb. He fell onto his chest.

A strong hand grabbed him by the shoulder and rolled him onto his back. His vision went black, but he felt a tiny, warm weight pressing on his chest. Pinpricks of pain followed the clawing trail up to his throat. His body was drifting away in a haze of numbness and pain, but he still felt the even scrape of a little tongue across the wound in his throat. Sharp teeth closed around the ragged flesh, tearing.

As he died, he thought about the truths of nature he had learned. He wondered if he still had more to learn, or if he had just learned the greatest truth of all. The final truth.

The Wife's Story

Ursula K. Le Guin

He was a good husband, a good father. I don't understand it. I
don't believe in it. I don't believe that it happened. I saw it happen
but it isn't true. It can't be. He was always gentle. If you'd have seen
him playing with the children, anybody who saw him with the children would have known that there wasn't any bad in him, not one
mean bone. When I first met him, he was still living with his mother over near Spring Lake, and I used to see them together, the mother and the sons, and think that any young fellow that was that nice
with his family must be one worth knowing. Then one time when I
was walking in the woods I met him by himself coming back from a
hunting trip. He hadn't got any game at all, not so much as a field
mouse, but he wasn't cast down about it. He was just larking along
enjoying the morning air. That's one of the things I first loved about
him. He didn't take things hard, he didn't grouch and whine when
things didn't go his way. So we got to talking that day. And I guess
things moved right along after that, because pretty soon he was over
here pretty near all the time. And my sister said—see, my parents had
moved out the year before and gone south, leaving us the place—my
sister said, kind of teasing but serious, "Well! If he's going to be here
every day and half the night, I guess there isn't room for me!" And
she moved out—just down the way. We've always been real close, her
and me. That's the sort of thing doesn't ever change. I couldn't ever
have got through this bad time without my sis.

Well, so he came to live here. And all I can say is, it was the happy
year of my life. He was just purely good to me. A hard worker and
never lazy, and so big and fine-looking. Everybody looked up to him,
you know, young as he was. Lodge-meeting nights, more and more
often they had him to lead the singing. He had such a beautiful
voice, and he'd lead off strong, and the others following and joining

77

in, high voices and low. It brings the shivers on me now to think of it, hearing it, nights when I'd stayed home from meeting when the children were babies—the singing coming up through the trees there, and the moonlight, summer nights, the full moon shining. I'll never hear anything so beautiful. I'll never know a joy like that again.

It was the moon, that's what they say. It's the moon's fault, and the blood. It was in his father's blood. I never knew his father, and now I wonder what become of him. He was from up Whitewater way, and had no kin around here. I always thought he went back there, but now I don't know. There was some talk about him, tales, that come out after what happened to my husband. It's something runs in the blood, they say, and it may never come out, but if it does, it's the change of the moon that does it. Always happens in the dark of the moon. When everybody's home asleep. Something comes over the one that's got the curse in his blood, they say, and he gets up because he can't sleep, and he goes out into the glaring sun, and goes off alone—drawn to find those like him. And it may be so, because my husband would do that. I'd half rouse and say, "Where you going to?" and he'd say, "Oh, hunting, be back this evening," and it wasn't like him, even his voice was different. But I'd be so sleepy, and not wanting to wake the kids, and he was so good and responsible, it was no call of mine to go asking "Why?" and "Where?" and all like that.

So it happened that way maybe three times or four. He'd come back late, and worn out, and pretty near cross for one so sweet-tempered—not wanting to talk about it. I figured everybody got to bust out now and then, and nagging never helped anything. But it did begin to worry me. Not so much that he went, but that he came back so tired and strange. Even, he smelled strange. It made my hair stand up on end. I could not endure it and I said, "What is that—those smells on you? All over you!" And he said, "I don't know," real short, and made like he was sleeping. But he went down when he thought I wasn't noticing, and washed and washed himself. But those smells stayed in his hair, and in our bed, for days.

And then the awful thing. I don't find it easy to tell about this. I want to cry when I have to bring it to my mind. Our youngest, the little one, my baby, she turned from her father. Just overnight. He come in and she got scared-looking, stiff, with her eyes wide, and then she begun to cry and try to hide behind me. She didn't yet talk plain but she was saying over and over, "Make it go away! Make it go away!"

The look in his eyes, just for one moment, when he heard that. That's what I don't want ever to remember. That's what I can't forget. The look in his eyes looking at his own child.

I said to the child, "Shame on you, what's got into you?"—scolding, but keeping her right up close to me at the same time, because I was frightened too. Frightened to shaking.

He looked away then and said something like, "Guess she just waked up dreaming," and passed it off that way. Or tried to. And so did I. And I got real mad with my baby when she kept on acting crazy scared of her own dad. But she couldn't help it and I couldn't change it.

He kept away that whole day. Because he knew, I guess. It was just beginning dark of the moon.

It was hot and close inside, and dark, and we'd all been asleep some while, when something woke me up. He wasn't there beside me. I heard a little stir in the passage when I listened. So I got up, because I could bear it no longer. I went out into the passage, and it was light there, hard sunlight coming in from the door. And I saw him standing just outside, in the tall grass by the entrance. His head was hanging. Presently, he sat down, like he felt weary, and looked down at his feet. I held still, inside, and watched—I didn't know what for.

And I saw what he saw. I saw the changing. In his feet, it was, first. They got long, each foot got longer, stretching out, the toes stretching out and the foot getting long, and fleshy, and white. And no hair on them.

The hair begun to come away all over his body. It was like his hair fried away in the sunlight and was gone. He was white all over, then, like a worm's skin. And he turned his face. It was changing while I looked. It got flatter and flatter, the mouth flat and wide, and the teeth grinning flat and dull, and the nose just a knob of flesh with nostril holes, and the ears gone, and the eyes gone blue—staring at me out of that flat, soft, white face.

He stood up then on two legs.

I saw him, I had to see him, my own dear love, turned into the hateful one.

I couldn't move, but as I crouched there in the passage staring out into the day, I was trembling and shaking with a growl that burst out into a crazy, awful howling. A grief howl and a terror howl and a calling howl. And the others heard it, even sleeping, and woke up.

It stared and peered, that thing my husband had turned into, and shoved its face up to the entrance of our house. I was still bound by mortal fear, but behind me the children had waked up, and the baby was whimpering. The mother anger come into me then, and I snarled and crept forward.

The man thing looked around. It had no gun, like the ones from the man places do. But it picked up a heavy fallen tree-branch in its long white foot, and shoved the end of that down into our house, at me. I snapped the end of it in my teeth and started to force my way out, because I knew the man would kill our children if it could. But my sister was already coming. I saw her running at the man with her head low and her mane high and her eyes yellow as the winter sun. It turned on her and raised up that branch to hit her. But I come out of the doorway, mad with the mother anger, and the others all were coming answering my call, the whole pack gathering, there in that blind glare and heat of the sun at noon.

The man looked around at us and yelled out loud, and brandished the branch it held. Then it broke and ran, heading for the cleared fields and plowlands, down the mountainside. It ran, on two legs, leaping and weaving, and we followed it.

I was last, because love still bound the anger and the fear in me. I was running when I saw them pull it down. My sister's teeth were in its throat. I got there and it was dead. The others were drawing back from the kill, because of the taste of the blood, and the smell. The younger ones were cowering and some crying, and my sister rubbed her mouth against her forelegs over and over to get rid of the taste. I went up close because I thought if the thing was dead, the spell, the curse, might be done, and my husband could come back—alive, or even dead, if I could only see him, my true love, in his true form, beautiful. But only the dead man lay there white and bloody. We drew back and back from it, and turned and ran, back up into the hills, back to the woods of the shadows and the twilight and the blessed dark.

Teamwork

Paul Allen

Gretchen's well-manicured fingers were in her lap, fidgeting with the marquise-cut solitaire on her right hand. "Well, are you ready to meet Lyka?" asked the trainer as she buzzed the intercom. "She's a real beauty; one hundred twenty-eight pounds and solid black."

"I thought pedigreed shepherds were tan and black. I didn't think to ask if you used purebreds."

"U.S. breeders have overbred German shepherds, so we had to find a strain of active working shepherds to restock our dog-guide program. We discovered that East German and Rumanian farmers still used working shepherds with their livestock. Farmers bred only enough to meet their own needs, not the needs of fancy dog show breeders. They guaranteed the purity of their shepherd gene pool. Six months ago, we got our first shipment from Rumania. You're the first student to team up with an animal from this new strain."

"Does she shed much?" asked Gretchen.

The trainer took a slow, deep breath. "Nearly all dogs shed, usually with the seasons."

"My wardrobe is full of light colors. And if she's black...well, I can have her bathed and groomed daily. That should minimize the side effect of dark fur on my wardrobe," said Gretchen, placing her hands palm down on her tight jeans.

"Bathing and grooming are not done to control 'side effects.' They're activities that foster team trust.

"This relationship will require something very different from what I imagine you're used to," persisted the trainer. "Your relationship with your dog guide isn't commercial. It's based on trust and intimacy. You and the dog are not drawing up a contract. The dog only works for the positive attention you willingly and consistently give it."

Gretchen smiled disarmingly. *If it sounds like a deal, and it feels like a deal, it's probably a deal.* "I'm sure you're right," she lied.

Butterflies stirred within Gretchen when she heard the attendant and the dog coming down the hall. "Remember," said the trainer, "let Lyka initiate contact. Everyone's been using this room, so it's full of interesting smells; you might not be of immediate interest. I've been training her intensively for six months. She knows me. Identifying the pack is the first priority; after that comes territory. By the time you leave here, you'll be part of the pack. Then, no matter where you go, Lyka will be more interested in staying by your side than exploring new territory."

Gretchen's heart thudded and her mouth grew dry. "I was hoping I wouldn't be so nervous after three days of basic training. I never dreamed I'd have to depend on a dog some day."

The door opened and a kennel attendant ushered the animal into the day room. Without a word, the attendant withdrew and closed the door behind him. Gretchen stiffened when the unleashed animal bounded around the room. She relaxed a little when the dog raced whimpering to greet the trainer. The dog snuggled the trainer, and Gretchen could hear the cuddling sounds as the trainer rough-housed the excited animal. "Oh, yes, Lyka, good morning to you, too," cooed the trainer. Waves of vague anxiety fluttered through Gretchen's stomach while she waited for the contact. She played with a section of her long, blond hair that fell across her upper shoulder.

"Whoa, forget the territory, here she comes, Gretchen." The trainer sounded surprised. "Keep your hands relaxed in your lap and speak her name gently." Gretchen did not want to reach out. "She's examining your shoes right now—probably smells other dog scents. Since she doesn't know you, she will want to determine the companions you hang with."

The dog sniffed at her legs from a safe distance. "Say hello and use her name."

"Hello, Lyka," Gretchen said without expression.

The inquisitive animal forced its hard muzzle under her hands and pressed its nose deeply into her crotch. Its massive ribcage expanded between Gretchen's knees as the dog inhaled deeply. Startled by Lyka's unexpected boldness, Gretchen flinched and the animal backed away. "Easy, Lyka," said the trainer. "She feels the need to dominate you. You're not opening up to her. Don't be mysterious."

"Does she do this to everyone she meets?"

"Not really," said the trainer with a clap of her hands. "Lyka, easy girl, you're not friends, not quite yet." Gretchen reached out a hand to touch the animal. She suppressed a cry as the beast lunged into her lap. It pinned her hands against her thighs with its front paws. Sharp claw points flexed into the skin at the back of both hands. Gretchen tried to free her hands, then froze. A blast of hot breath struck her full in the face. A rumbling, deep-throated growl warned her of the danger that towered over her, half on the floor, half on her lap.

"Calm down, Lyka," called the trainer. "She's decided to dominate you. Don't let yourself be intimidated. Say hello so she doesn't get the idea you're submissive."

"Good morning, Lyka," Gretchen said timidly. The animal whined softly when it heard its name and, without further concern, washed Gretchen's face with its broad tongue. Lyka returned to the floor and tried to snuggle into the blind woman's arms. Gretchen used the back of both hands to wipe the saliva from her cheeks and forehead.

"Wow," said the trainer. "That was fast. Guess you two belong together now. Lyka seems to have accepted you."

The shepherd casually smelled Gretchen's armpit. Sniffing its way down her arm, she showed keen interest in Gretchen right hand. She gingerly licked at the back of the hand, and then continued to sniff. The trainer walked over to Gretchen. "Let's see what she's inspecting."

"Perhaps she's not interested in me. Maybe she's attracted to investment-grade diamonds," the blind woman said, refolding her hands into her lap.

"Oh, she's found a cut on the back of your hand," said the trainer, ignoring the remark. "She probably nicked you when she jumped onto your lap."

"Is it bleeding much?" asked Gretchen as she showed the hand to the other woman. Unconsciously, Gretchen scratched behind Lyka's ear with her left hand.

"No, it's fine. Although when you wiped your face, some of the blood streaked across your left cheek. The two of you are bonded for good now. Lyka's lineage is so close to original wolf lines that she probably maintains many wolf characteristics."

"You don't mean a taste for blood?" quipped Gretchen.

"No. She's too domesticated for that. I mean her senses of taste and smell are so beyond those of ordinary dogs that she can probably detect and identify variations within blood samples. She doesn't seem to mind yours though."

"If she accepts me, then I'm glad she has good taste," laughed Gretchen, her fingers examining the astonishing length of the exposed canine fangs protruding past the dog's lower lip.

"In a way, Lyka now knows you more intimately than she knows me. She's never tasted my blood to my knowledge."

Gretchen hesitated while reflecting on that thought. "What if she senses I'm still afraid after a while?"

"The dog already senses your feelings. Any change inside you is going to be obvious to Lyka. Over time, the two of you will thoroughly bond, and then Lyka will sense the improvement in your working relationship. She'll know that you no longer fear her and the trust will strengthen your team work even more."

"But what if she still doesn't like me...I mean, after a while." Lyka sat between Gretchen's legs and rested her head on the woman's lap. Gretchen stroked the unusually long, lush fur that covered the animal's spine and ribs.

"What's not to like? Besides, after fifteen years of running a luxury car dealership, I'm sure you could sell anything to anyone once you've made up your mind. Sell yourself to Lyka. And when you and Lyka get your act together, you'll have the mobility you need to continue running your business."

"I've never felt so afraid of everything in my life," Gretchen confessed. "What if I can't run my business anymore? What if the dog isn't enough?" Gretchen felt her eyes moisten. "I spend too much time wishing I could still see."

"One step at a time, Gretchen. You've got three weeks of harness training before you leave here. There'll be plenty of time to develop a bond of trust before the two of you return home."

Simon decelerated the Mercedes SL600 convertible as they approached Gretchen's estates. For the past twenty minutes, she'd been gritting her teeth nonstop. Insisting on putting the convertible's top down did nothing to keep him quiet. He simply raised his voice to shout over the noise of highway traffic. She envied Lyka's position: hang your head out of the car and let the wind inform your nose and shut down your hearing. Simon continued to chatter. She wondered if she could stand the final two-minute trip up her private drive.

"There's a full moon tonight," continued Simon. Gretchen heard Lyka sniffing the air as she lay down in the back seat. "Beautiful night for a walk." Gretchen twisted her head to face the door. Lyka had leaned forward and was sniffing the hair behind Gretchen's left ear.

"Would you like to take a walk? We really need to chat, Gretchen." Simon's tone was anxious and not well controlled. "Why are you turning away from me?" Simon whimpered.

"I'm not turning away," Gretchen snapped. "I just don't want any more of Lyka's drool in my hair." Lyka stood up in the back seat when the car rolled to a stop in front of the main verandah. "And no, Simon. No walks in the moonlight. We've been over this countless times."

"I don't mind running the morning meetings for you for a while, 'til…" Simon began. Gretchen opened the car door, got out and slammed the door shut.

"Here, Lyka," she commanded. Lyka stood on the back seat obediently as Gretchen felt for the leash clipped to the dog's choke collar.

"We've got to talk," whined Simon. "For God's sake, I've been driving you to and from work for a week now, and…" Holding the leash, Gretchen commanded Lyka, "Come!" Gracefully, the large shepherd obeyed and jumped from the plush leather to the smooth cobblestone.

"God damn it, Simon," growled Gretchen. "Stop pressuring me." Facing Simon, she spoke quietly, leaning against the body of the open convertible. "I know you've been pulling more than your share of the dealership while I get my feet under me with Lyka. I do realize it, and I appreciate it. I've also never lied to you about my feelings, Simon. I am not in love with you, and I do not want that kind of relationship."

She and Lyka climbed the broad flagstone steps leading up to the verandah. She turned toward the idling car below. "Please take the 911 Turbo from my garage back to the showroom. Have the Porsche readied for sale. I'll take four percent less than usual without compromising the sales commission. Leave the six hundred where it is."

"Wait, I'll give you the keys," Simon said, opening the driver's door.

"No, I want them left in the ignition. Thank you." She crossed the verandah to the front door of her formal entry. "I'll run Monday's meeting," she called over her shoulder. "Good night, Simon. Have a good weekend."

As Gretchen undressed, Lyka paced around the bedroom. Gretchen drained her first double Scotch, poured a second, and ran hot water for a relaxing soak.

Removing the large diamond ring, she opened the carved lid of an ebony jewelry box. The polished wood felt cool under her fingers. She traced the intricate lily carvings on the lid's surface. Although she had purchased the box years earlier, she observed the detail in greater depth with her hands than she ever had with her eyes. Placing the ring inside, she closed the lid and pushed the box against the other jewelry cases that were grouped together on her teak dresser.

One of the cases in the back clicked against the lower frame of the gilt antique mirror that spanned the width of the dresser. Pulling the case away from the mirror, she inadvertently touched the surface of the glass. She ignored the impulse to take a tissue and wipe away the fingerprint smudge. *Hell,* thought Gretchen, *it's not like I use the mirror anyway.* She finished her second double and closed herself in the bathroom.

After a long, steamy soak, Gretchen toweled herself dry and used a blow drier on her clean hair. She was too tired to brush it out tonight. After a week back at work, she just wanted to crawl off to bed. Lyka greeted her enthusiastically as she opened her bathroom door. Gretchen ignored the dog and walked into the dressing area. As she slipped her arms into the sleeves of her silk nightgown, Lyka put her cold nose against the still damp hair at Gretchen's groin.

"Lyka, no," said Gretchen irritably as she lowered her hands to push the dog's nose away from her body. Her hands closed on the animal's muzzle and felt the leather leash that draped from both sides of her mouth. "Oh, I get it," laughed Gretchen. "It's pee time, eh?"

Lyka surrendered the leash to her mistress and playfully bolted to the other side of the room. "Lyka, no," said Gretchen sharply. "I'm too tired for this. Lyka, come." She patted her left thigh just below the silk hem of her nightgown. Lyka ran and sat to her left. Clipping the leash to the choke chain, she led Lyka out past the back terrace to the expanse of manicured lawn behind the house. When they returned to the terrace, Lyka sat abruptly.

"Come on, girl," sighed Gretchen. "I'm not taking a walk in the moonlight with you, either. Let's get inside." She pulled on the leash. The dog stayed seated and resisted the tugging. "Lyka, damn it, I'm tired. I don't want to stand around out here." She stepped ahead of the dog and forcefully snapped the leash taut. Something clattered loudly against the tiles of the terrace. Lyka remained seated.

"What are you up to, Lyka?" She knelt at the animal's side and, with her free hand, felt around the area. Immediately ahead of the sitting Lyka, she found the dog's brush and comb. "Damn, you tricked me, didn't you? You brought these out here," Gretchen shouted. Lyka's tail swept the tile behind her and she licked Gretchen's neck. "Okay, okay. I just took a bath. Quit slobbering on me."

Removing the choke and leash from Lyka's neck, she dropped them to the ground and retrieved the grooming tools. "I'm really tired, so let's make this quick," muttered Gretchen. "I guess I can do this without being sober."

Tufts of loose fur floated from the metal comb as Gretchen vigorously ran it over Lyka's back and flanks. As she continued to groom more and more excess fur from her coat, it seemed that Lyka's dimensions had altered. Telling her "stay," she put down the brush and examined Lyka with both hands.

Lyka's neck appeared thinner. The ridge at her back wasn't as noticeable. Her back was broader at the shoulders and tapered to a distinct waist with wider hips, and all four legs seemed thicker than usual. The dog's coat felt loose on its body. Excess folds of pelt now hung underneath her. Probing the sagging skin with her fingers, Gretchen found that Lyka's belly felt bloated, fuller than normal. Working forward, she realized that the ribcage was shaped more like her own than that of a dog's.

"What the hell is going on?" The ground slowly spun beneath her. Then there came an agonizing sound of something ripping. Gretchen sat back on her heels for balance. There was a rhythmic sound of dripping liquid, and a faint sputtering like wet, frothy gasping. Gretchen felt dizzy. The taste of bile flowed from her throat into her mouth. She spit out the bitter liquid and gagged.

"Lyka, help me!" Slipping onto her hands and knees, she felt forward with one hand. The tile under the animal was covered by an enormous pelt of wet fur. Her fingers came away coated with thick mucus. She reached out to touch Lyka. Instead of lush fur, she found a mucus-like slime. Beneath the thin film, she felt the texture of skin.

"Oh, no, Lyka! What's happening to you?" Gretchen moved her hand toward the dog's mouth. "Oh God, I think I'm going to be sick." Her fingers first got tangled in a mass of long, thick, wet tresses. Human hair.

Following the hair, she found a broad, vaulted forehead; two forward-projecting eye sockets separated by a thin, aquiline nose; and high cheekbones. *God, it's a human face!* The head convulsed slightly under her touch. Wiping mucus off the face and mouth changed the wet sound into ragged breathing. With the lightest touch, Gretchen ran her hands down across the wet torso. Distinct, angular shoulder blades were protruding from the broad back…and two breasts, as large as Gretchen's own, hung below the flattened chest wall. Gretchen reached for the woman's throat and searched for a pulse.

"Lyka, come here now," she cried out. The dog didn't respond.

"Lyka!" Gretchen flinched, pulling her hand away when the woman stirred and turned her face toward Gretchen.

"Here I am. Give me a few minutes, I'm getting there." Lyka's voice was deep-chested, but richly feminine. It sounded like a rustling of dried leaves, of wind, of slow running water—a voice that drew her, commanded her full attention, compelled her to listen.

"What in the name of God," Gretchen whispered as she stood, shaking violently.

"Hang on, Gretchen," Lyka said as she staggered onto her two legs. "I've only ever done this in front of a few hundred sheep!" She cleared her throat, spitting thick mucus out from deep within her throat. "I'm new to this 'dog-guide' business. Never been used like that before. It's rough keeping up with the changes." Lyka made the moaning sound of someone luxuriating in a thorough stretch.

Gretchen raised a hand and massaged her right temple. "A dog turning into a woman?"

"You mean a wolf into a woman, don't you?"

Gretchen shivered as the thought crossed her mind. "This isn't possible."

"A wolf can turn into a human just as easily as a human into a wolf. They call it lycanthropy."

"You mean you aren't human?"

"Whatever is bitten by a were-animal becomes a were-animal. I was a Rumanian shepherd trying to protect my master from an attack when I was bitten. My master escaped. I alone received 'the gift'." Lyka took Gretchen's hand firmly in hers and led the blind woman toward the house. "Come on, I'm freezing. Let's go inside. Let's have some cognac. You do have cognac, don't you?"

Completely numb, Gretchen allowed herself to be led into the house. "No, I don't drink brandy. I only have Scotch, but it's over seventy years old."

"Where do we go to find this 'Scotch'?"

"It's in my...bedroom."

When Gretchen released Lyka's hand, Lyka began pacing around the bedroom. "I've enjoyed this past week. You live very, very well." The sound of her pleasure was running through her voice. "And I haven't driven a Mercedes since Prague in '68." Lyka went to the bar. Two glasses clinked together, followed by the pop of a cork stopper and twin rushes of liquid. Lyka brought the drinks over to where Gretchen stood and slipped a six-ounce glass full of Scotch into Gretchen's extended hand. "I've never enjoyed transforming into a woman and finding myself in a dog shelter in the middle of a Rumanian winter with forty-eight hours to kill."

"What do you want, Lyka?"

"Let me share my secret with you."

Gretchen walked over to her velvet loveseat, sat down, and took a large swallow of Scotch. "You don't have anything I want, and you are not staying. Besides, I'm not interested in living with anyone."

"You already are. Lyka the dog guide is with you twenty-eight days a month. I'm here only two days a month." Lyka walked over to Gretchen's dresser. "This is a beautiful mirror. Seventeenth century, I believe. Cornwall." Lyka sipped her drink.

"Stop looking at my things. I don't need your appreciation of my antiques."

"Perhaps," Lyka purred, "I've overestimated your powers of observation. I can leave here and immediately replace your luxuries with those of someone else. You can get another dog guide. But that other dog guide can't give you what I'm offering. Do you know anyone—and I do mean anyone—who, with one bite, could grant you your fondest wish within the span of several heartbeats?"

Lyka's voice was even, but quiet. "Last time. What do you desire most?"

The silence in the room thundered in Gretchen's ears. "I don't want..."

"You don't want…"

"Get away from the mirror, God damn it!" Gretchen rose to her feet. Lyka wheeled around to face her.

"What about the mirror, Gretchen?" The glass in Gretchen's hand began shaking, spilling liquor onto the Persian rug.

"I want you to leave. Now."

"Answer me, Gretchen."

With a sudden move, Gretchen flung the glass at Lyka, screaming at the top of her lungs, "Get out! Get out! Get out!" With an ear-splitting crash, the glass shattered the mirror into thousands of showering fragments.

Then silence.

"Killing the messenger doesn't change the truth of the message. Tell me, Gretchen, did you break the mirror so I couldn't use it? Or did you break it because you can't use it?"

Gretchen's arms hung limply at her sides. Tears began rolling down her cheeks. "Damn you," she whispered hoarsely.

"Too late," Lyka retorted. She retrieved a dirty hand towel from the hamper and proceeded to wipe glass shards off the jewelry boxes. Both women remained silent. Lyka took a makeup mirror from the dressing table and placed it on the dresser.

Gretchen's voice trembled. "What do I have to do to regain my eyesight?"

"It's all very easy. I bite you. It's like an injection, really. The lycanthropy spreads through your circulatory system, transforming your metabolism, making it sensitive to the lunar cycle." Lyka opened the box and began sorting through the jewelry.

"Do you do anything disgusting? I mean, do you drink my blood?"

"I'm too domesticated for that," Lyka snorted while holding a double strand of lustrous black pearls up to her neck.

"Does the bite leave a scar?"

"How vain you are." Lyka smiled at the beautiful, black-haired, oval-faced reflection in the small makeup mirror. "Since I'm not rabid, and this isn't an infection, the wound heals cleanly. You know, these black pearls set off my green eyes beautifully."

"But lycanthropy—werewolfism—is a disease, isn't it? It must have side effects."

"It's no disease," Lyka said dreamily, holding up a stunning pair of three-quarter-karat emerald earrings. "It's a transfiguring opportunity, but I suppose you could say that getting your eyesight back is one hell of a side effect."

"Then what?"

"Then, nothing."

"What happens during those two days?" Gretchen persisted.

"Nothing. We simply enjoy ourselves." Lyka turned smoothly to face the other woman. "For two days a month, I am able to be human. For two days a month, you'll have keen eyesight."

"Where do you bite me?"

"Any large muscle. Slip off your gown."

Gretchen announced her decision with a whispering of silk.

Lyka now stood in front of Gretchen. "Get on all fours," she said softly.

Gretchen hesitated. "Does it hurt?"

Lyka moved closer to her, lightly scratching the skin over Gretchen's sternum, sensing the overwhelming hunger within her. "Yes and no," Lyka said gently.

Lyka lightly drew her nails downward, starting at the notch in Gretchen's collar bones, stroking between her breasts to her navel, then returned the stroke upward to her throat. "I can show you things you have seen before, Gretchen. I can also show you things you have never seen. The choice is yours. The decision is yours. I can only offer."

Gretchen lowered herself to her hands and knees. Lyka knelt alongside her and ran her hands from the small of Gretchen's back to the base of her scalp. Gretchen shivered as the skin tightened over her ribs. Her chest was flooded with a warm tingling sensation. Lyka repeated the motion several times. Gretchen began to feel the warmth moving from her chest to her upper abdomen. Her breathing came faster.

When Lyka's soft hands reached Gretchen's neck one last time, she gathered the long blond hair and pulled it over the top of Gretchen's head, exposing the woman's slender neck. Lyka placed her open mouth on the back of Gretchen's neck and moistened the skin with her tongue. Slowly, she drew her mouth down the gasping woman's backbone. When she reached her hip, Lyka gently massaged the hip muscle with her front upper canines and sharp incisors. Perspiration trickled down Gretchen's face. She threw her head back but stifled the cry as Lyka sank her teeth deep into the muscle. Lyka chewed gently, keeping her teeth firmly in the wound. Gretchen wept with release, lowering her head and continuing to weep as Lyka withdrew from her flesh.

Lyka led Gretchen to the passenger side and opened the door. Gretchen seated herself, and Lyka closed the door behind her. Lyka's legs and buttocks tingled as she slid her naked skin into the leather driver's seat. She fired the SL600's ignition, reveling in the feel of the four hundred horsepower, twelve-cylinder engine as it roared to life. She saw Gretchen carefully studying the house.

"Sight's a wonderful thing, isn't it?" Lyka allowed the tachometer to drop below one thousand r.p.m. Gretchen turned to Lyka and pressed her muzzle against the woman's neck. The blond shepherd licked Lyka behind her right ear, and Lyka laughed, stroking the long, platinum-blond fur on Gretchen's chest.

"Feels good, doesn't it? A small pat here, a major scratch there," she said as she eased the vehicle out onto the main road. "The pack has its advantages."

Gretchen curled her bulk tightly into the bucket seat. She rested her head on the doorframe, aiming her nose into the wind current. As the coupe picked up speed, Lyka stroked Gretchen's warm flank. "Wolf senses are nice, but human senses do have their advantages. I can tell that both of us are going to enjoy this arrangement."

Inhaling deeply, Gretchen hung her head outside and lost herself to the moonlit landscape and the perfumes of the approaching dawn.

Sisters of the Weird

Thomas S. Roche

I was on summer break from the state college, and living with my parents in their condo out on Highway XX. Well, I guess it's just like any place else in the country, probably even where you live. Daddy, God bless him, was working long hours at the arms-manu-facturing plant and working so hard with the Shriners to build that hospital in the next county for the nuns and orphans. Or something like that. Mom, meanwhile, kept herself busy driving around in her pink Cadillac with her white poodle, Fifi, selling makeup, Tupperware and garage-door openers. She was pretty good at it, a self-made woman.

Mom was intent on making sure I got a job that summer.

"Get a job!" she would snarl, breathing smoke around the lip-stick-stained butt of a Virginia Slim. "No daughter of mine is gonna spend the summer lounging around the house all day in her under-wear and then whoring around with every Tom, Dick and Harry until the wee hours of the morning! Isn't Drool Burger hiring?"

"Elizabeth, you're getting hysterical," said Dad, without looking away from the TV. He was watching the Fiesta's wet T-shirt contest on that weird public access station. Some people are so strange. "Besides," he said, "I thought that guy's name was Butch."

"Butch dumped her—will you show a little concern for your daughter? Butch dumped her for some degenerate." Mom patted Fifi and smiled, as if pleased with herself.

I was barely listening. "Mom, I can't work at Drool Burger. My skin will break out."

"Well, then what about Fiesta's Bar, next to the Frozen Food Emporium? They had a sign in the window. Jenny Wollerson's mom—you know Jenny—she told me so, said they had a sign up that they were hiring. Didn't they have a sign up they were hiring?

I'm sure that's what they said. They're hiring. I think you could go over there and get a job."

"Mom, I can't work at a bar, I'm only nineteen."

"Isn't that a biker place?" asked Dad. His face was turning red and he looked very uncomfortable.

"That's okay, you can use my ID and say you're forty-six. We look almost exactly alike if you bleach your hair. I'm sure they'll hire you, Virginia, a pretty girl like you? You'll look *good* in one of those uniforms, won't she Larry? They're so flattering to the girlish figure! I'm sure they'll give you the job, no problem! Can you get me free drinks if I come in when it's not busy?"

I guess Mom had a point. I was kind of depressed last summer because of Butch. I had really loved him. I even had the wedding all planned in my head. I used to sit there in Economics, humming the wedding march and envisioning the beautiful peach-colored bridesmaid dresses. It made me sad just thinking about it. Butch was captain of the football team and student body president at State U. A double major in Literature and Economics, he wanted to be the president of a corporation, drive a BMW and write the Great American Novel. He had great shoulders. We made love for the first time (my first time) under the light of the full moon on the south field at the edge of campus. I liked it a lot, even though he kept trying to recite poetry in my ear while we were doing it, and I kept shushing him. Afterwards, the mist came in off the river and hovered around us, like that one scene from *Trailer Park Massacre*, only it wasn't scary at all—it was beautiful, and very romantic. Then, these deer came along and nibbled at the grass right beside us, and I heard dogs howling far away. I had this feeling that I was totally connected to nature or something freaky like that. I told Butch about it, and I guess that was my first hint that he might not be as nice a guy as I thought he was. He told me to get a life. Jeez, he was the one reciting Byron.

But Butch told me a bunch of stuff that made me feel really special, so I didn't know what to believe. I guess I was pretty naïve.

Butch dumped me on the same day that I found out I flunked Econ. He said he wanted to go out with a girl with...well, someone bustier. Can you imagine? What an asshole. I would have given anything to get him back.

Mom did as she promised; she gave me her ID and I went down

to Fiesta's. The owner's name was Freddy Puzo. He was from upstate New York and he wore an apron, no matter how filthy it was, even when he left the bar. He smiled when I told him my name was Virginia. Like it meant something. "That's a nice name, Virginia." He told me he had bought the place from some Mexicans. People always came in looking for margaritas because of the name of the bar. "You tell them, at Freddy's we don't serve none of those Mexican fag drinks. Jesus, it's not like this is L.A. or Cabo San Lucas or some damn thing. This is an American bar." He was going to get the sign changed to *Freddy's Bar* as soon as he could find a sign shop that would do it for free. *Whatever,* I thought. Freddy didn't even ask to see Mom's ID. I just told him I was forty-six and he nodded and said, "Okay. You gotta be twenty-one to serve drinks. I wasn't born yesterday, you know. Heck, neither were you; you know what I'm talking about. You're a pretty girl." He winked.

Whatever, I thought to myself.

There were only two other waitresses for this whole big place that served drinks and munchies and had live entertainment, so we kept pretty busy. We had to wear these outfits: tight and really short skirts, like really short, in one-hundred-percent stretch polyester; these tight bowling shirts that said *Freddy's Bar* on the back in flowery script; and these really bizarre two-foot-tall hats that looked like giant blue bananas with red and orange stripes and fuzzy balls hanging in front of your face. And for some reason, the top two buttons on all the uniform shirts were gone, like they had been cut off. We all just safety-pinned the shirts closed.

The other waitresses who worked at Freddy's were Maddy and Chartreuse. Maddy is maybe ten years or so older than me, though a lot younger than forty-six; she smokes Pall Malls constantly and can cuss up a mean streak. I once saw a drunk biker try to grab her ass. Whew, that guy won't be riding bareback anytime soon. Maddy has a tattoo of a dagger just above her left breast; she showed it to me when we were changing one time. She said she had a better one on her ass, and I could see it sometime if I was really good. It seemed strange that I had to be good to see the tattoo on her ass, but I had no plans for being especially bad, so I just smiled and nodded and said, "Okay." In some ways, she was even stranger than Freddy.

Chartreuse is this wispy little thing that weighs maybe eighty-five pounds if she is holding a full tray of drinks and wearing lead panties.

She has jet black hair and kind of blue-white skin. She is really weird looking, but kind of neat, like a younger and sweeter Morticia Addams. You can see the veins in her throat, which I think is pretty cool. She didn't say much, but sometimes she giggled when Maddy would say something really outrageous. Chartreuse seemed like a harmless little girl, but one night after our shift, she opened her backpack and showed me this really big gun. Like really, really big.

"It's a forty-four auto-mag, eight round clip. Just like Dirty Harry used," she giggled. Her eyes lit up with glee. "Hope that biker tries to grab *my* ass one of these days."

Mom and Dad came into Fiesta's once, and Mom seemed really freaked out. She didn't know the place was so sleazy when she told me to get a job there. But she still wanted free drinks. I paid Freddy for Mom's drinks out of my tips, and—Sweet Francesca! (as Freddy would say, I think it's the name of his dead wife)—that woman could put 'em away.

Some nights, things got pretty strange, worst of all when they had these wet T-shirt contests on the first of each month with these girls from the next county. They would bring in blond centerfold models, a year younger than me, and make them put on these brand new Fruit-of-the-Looms and squirt them with seltzer water. Maddy would just stand there watching in between drawing pitchers at the bar. She would shake her head, puffing on an unfiltered Pall Mall and muttering angrily to herself. Sometimes I was kind of glad she wasn't packing heat like Chartreuse.

Freddy's attracted this cross of truckers, really mainstream guys (like aluminum-siding salesmen and Fuller-brush men) and Hell's Angels. They were all pretty rude. But then again, I couldn't figure out what they were talking about half the time, with lines like "I think I'll have one of you—make it two!" when I asked them what they wanted, and "Is that a blue banana on your head, or are you just glad to see me?" Like no one had ever thought of those jokes before; they made as little sense one night as they had the night before. Sometimes guys are just really weird.

Eventually I got the picture from Maddy that these guys were just trying to piss me off. I still didn't understand why they'd come on to me by asking stupid questions from Mars, but I took Maddy's advice and just ignored them. Maddy did tell me, though, that if any guy tried to grab me, I should let her know, and we'd just see whether he'd have one of me, make it two, or if he would suddenly find that one borderline sociopath bar dyke was using her spike heel to turn his diseased schlong into a slightly undercooked corn dog. And he'd better hope it wasn't a full moon.

Chartreuse giggled when Maddy said that. I didn't quite get the corn dog reference. But I felt safe knowing that Maddy was going to take care of me if some asshole tried to put his hand up my skirt. It made me like her more than ever. She was really cool.

Maybe that's why she and I started hanging out together after work. I mean, there wasn't much to do at three in the morning, so we'd go to the Diner Garden Moonlight Café on Highway XX and drink coffee 'til the sun came up. Chartreuse would come along, but she didn't say much. She just kept opening her backpack and looking in, and smiling to herself. Sometimes she would giggle.

The waitress who worked graveyard at the Moonlight was named Bubbles. She was about a hundred years old and had a beehive that hit the light fixtures if she didn't dip down when she went under them. She wore an awful lot of makeup. She was a really nice old woman. The cook was this nice black guy who sometimes came out and chatted with us, since there weren't a lot of flapjacks to be made at three in the morning. Mostly, though, me and Maddy and Chartreuse just hung out together and drank coffee and sometimes ate fries.

Maddy had a hard life. Her parents died when she was still in high school so she had to marry her boyfriend Mitch who was a dog boy in a circus. I didn't think that was a very nice thing to say about an old flame, but I'd called Butch a few things like "prickface" and "shiteater" before, so I could kind of relate. Then I figured out that she was serious; he was a dog boy. I saw it on *Nova* once. He taught her lots of things. Mitch and Maddy even had a baby girl together. Then one day Mitch and the baby were both hit by a runaway clown car—you know, one of those tiny cars with, like, fifty clowns crammed inside (I always figured it must be hard to drive like that)—while they were napping in the tent. Both of them were killed instantly.

"At least they didn't suffer, but it damn near killed me, too," said Maddy, fighting back her tears. "I started smoking crack, hitchhiking, wandering from town to town. Christ, I was only sixteen, what did I know? Thank God I always used rubbers."

She got hooked up with some guy name Killer Bonaparte, who held up liquor stores for a living. "He was a dog boy like Mitch," said Maddy, her voice shaking. "But he was a different sort of dog boy. You wouldn't notice it to look at him, but he had longer fangs. He worshiped...the Dark Side of the Moon." She looked at me pointedly. "Do you know what I mean?"

"Oh yeah," I said. "Yeah, definitely." That was a really great album, Butch and I made it to that album once. He put it on repeat on his CD player. It was the only time I'd gotten stoned.

Maddy went on. She told me Killer Bonaparte was the cruellest name she'd ever heard. I had to agree with her on that one. He kept Maddy filled up with drugs and tricks, took her hunting with him. "But then Killer tried to take a swing at me one day." Maddy leaned really close. "It's not true about the silver bullet." I didn't know what she was talking about—I figured she meant that commercial, but I didn't see what her point was—I just let it pass since it was such a good story and I didn't want to interrupt. It was all so sad. "Anyway, that's when I finally quit drugs and men, and I never looked back."

"Wow," I told her. "What an incredible life story. Sounds like things have been really tough..."

"I get by," shrugged Maddy.

I thought about it for a long while, and none of us spoke. Then I broke the silence. "Whew. Whoopee on the men thing," I said. "I can go along with that, all right. This guy I knew at school, he and me, well, we were a thing for most of the year, I even went to bed with him."

Maddy's eyes went wide and the skin of her lips drew taut. She looked vaguely nauseous, and Chartreuse started giggling uncontrollably. Then Maddy laughed, too, but it was a really nervous kind of laughter, like she'd eaten something bad.

Chartreuse said, "Oh, Maddy, you've got such a weak stomach!"

Chartreuse winked at me and I just sort of smiled, not sure what was going on. You know when something unusual is happening, but you're not sure what? Like when you're a little kid and your parents won't tell you about some dumb sexual joke some idiot comedian made on TV? That's what it was like. Only it didn't bother me as much, seeing as it was Maddy and Chartreuse, and I was happy just to be with them.

That's when Maddy leaned really close to me and asked if I wanted to go back to their trailer up in the hills and have a drink. "I make one hell of a Tom Collins," she said, "and then we can take you out in the woods."

I said I didn't know she and Chartreuse lived together. "Well," said Maddy, "we try to keep it quiet, you know?" She winked at me.

I'm not really sure where to start with this part of it. See, I'd known all along there was something about Maddy and Chartreuse that didn't quite add up, but I wasn't sure what it was. I got this tingling feeling like I was about to find out. I wondered if they were into drugs or something. We got into Maddy's car, which was this really ancient Plymouth Valiant like my Uncle Joe used to drive, and Chartreuse sat in the back cradling her backpack lovingly. Maddy lit up a Pall Mall and squealed her tires pulling out of the parking lot. She drove really fast heading up into the hills. It made me kind of nervous but I liked it.

They lived a pretty long way from the bar, right on the county line. Their place was really tiny and kind of run down, but they kept it clean. While the two of them puttered in the kitchen, I sat down in the living room and leafed through a few of their books, which were mostly these artsy black and white photo books that my Mom would have had a fit about. "Those are Chartreuse's photo books," said Maddy as she handed me a Tom Collins in a plastic cup. "Chartreuse went to art school when she was younger. We keep all the *good* books in the bedroom." She smiled and winked lasciviously. "Come on, let's go outside. There are only a few more hours of darkness left." We took our drinks with us.

Chartreuse had left her backpack behind, and when I asked her about it, she smiled and said she wouldn't need it. They left the trailer unlocked and started on this trail, into the trees. There was this rich, clean piney smell you don't get down in the valley, even though we were only a half hour out of town. Plus you could see all the stars. It felt kind of like the night Butch and I made love in that field. Thinking about it made me kind of sad, but then Maddy reached over and squeezed my shoulder.

"It's beautiful," I told her.

Maddy just nodded and then kissed me on the forehead. From anyone else, it would have seemed like a really strange gesture, but from Maddy, it was totally natural. My heart started beating really fast, and I noticed how loud the crickets were chirping. In the distance, I could hear a wolf howling.

Maddy and Chartreuse both stopped, cocked their heads and listened. Another wolf joined the first. Then they both smiled.

"Mabel and Eileen," they said together.

We walked on for a bit longer, and I kept looking around. Maddy and Chartreuse seemed to know these woods perfectly, and Maddy had her hand on my shoulder, guiding me. I started thinking about how much I liked the woods and how peaceful they made me feel, when in her backwoods accent Chartreuse said, "We're here."

We'd come into this grove, a small flat clearing in the shape of a perfect circle. There were a couple of rocks on the edge, but mostly it was just a little field of overgrown grass. Maddy and Chartreuse finished their drinks and walked over to the middle, and I sort of hovered on the edge, watching them. Maddy turned to me, and I swear to God, I had never seen a woman as beautiful as she looked there in the middle of the night with the almost-full moon and all the stars lit up and shining down on her face. It made me want to recite Byron to her. I just stood there breathing fast.

"The moon doesn't have to be full all the way," said Maddy, "It's plenty close enough now. Stop us if we scare you."

With that, Maddy started unbuttoning her shirt. She took it off and unhitched her bra and tossed them both on the ground. Chartreuse was taking off her clothes, too, and her body was all white and pasty and I could see her blue veins even in the moonlight. Chartreuse was totally beautiful in her own way, too. Maddy kicked off her shoes and slid off her jeans, and she wasn't wearing anything underneath. The two of them were standing there naked together, looking at me. I just stood still, not sure what to think. Maddy reached out and touched Chartreuse on the cheek—affectionately, like you might do to your sister (that is, if you liked your sister an awful lot). But then they kissed on the lips, and it looked like it meant more than Butch had ever meant when he kissed me. They hugged each other, then pulled apart, still holding hands. Then the two of them looked up at the sky and stretched out their arms. I said I had never seen a woman as beautiful as Maddy in the moonlight. But she was a million times more beautiful naked in the moonlight, and Chartreuse had taken on a ghostly quality that made her seem just as beautiful and powerful, if not more so. I only wished I had been the one kissing Maddy—but I knew better than to be jealous.

I could see that Maddy really did have a tattoo on her ass, but I couldn't make it out at a distance.

That's when I heard the first howl, and it felt like the hair on the back of my neck stood up.

Maddy started it. Her mouth opened wide, and I swear, the sound that came out of it couldn't have been human. There's just no way. Then Chartreuse matched it, throwing her head back and howling like a dog or a wolf, louder than I could imagine her ever doing. I suddenly felt afraid but I didn't want them to stop. Something was raging inside me: I wanted to see what was going to happen, but at the same time, I knew this could be the end of everything. But Maddy and Chartreuse weren't the ones who could hurt me. Maddy howled again. As she shook her head back and forth, her hair flew everywhere, lit up by the moonlight. I closed my eyes, hearing the sound and feeling like it was a song. I could hear the other wolves matching the song, howling far away. When I opened my eyes, Chartreuse had dropped down onto her hands and knees, and her howling was louder than ever. Then Maddy was down, too, and they were barking and howling, all over each other, playing like puppies, and I couldn't believe what I was seeing. I thought maybe it was just the moonlight, a trick of the stars, like the way they twinkle or something. I started to shake.

The whole forest was alive with the howling now, far away, closer, everywhere. Wolves must have been matching that sound for thirty miles. They were making a sweet, terrifying song that couldn't have been coming from human throats. Half of me wanted to cry from fear, and half of me felt like this was the most beautiful thing I had ever seen or heard.

Then all of a sudden, the fear was gone and I could feel the moonlight raining down on me, like I had been freezing cold and was suddenly in a warm shower. It seemed silly to be standing in the shower in my clothes.

Maddy was more than an animal. She was like some sort of goddess screaming and yowling at the moon. I never would have thought I could understand her like that, up close. I felt her licking my face and her teeth grabbing at my throat as she pushed me down, and she growled like she was going to kill me. But I knew even as she bit me that I was totally safe, safer than I had ever been, and I would never be anything but. The moon had somehow become full in the middle of it all, and later Chartreuse told me that the moon is always full. It just depends on where you are.

Afterwards, we lay on our backs and held hands in a circle in the middle of the clearing, our hoarse voices howling quietly, sweetly. Maddy's hair was scattered around my face and I could smell it, musty and wonderful. All three of us were covered with dirt and grass but I didn't care. I started reciting Byron like Butch had done that one time, just the first stanza, and it fit perfectly. I said I had never seen anything more beautiful than Maddy naked under that howling moon, but that dawn breaking through the trees came pretty close.

Lying there, I got to thinking about this thing I saw on TV that really affected me when I was a kid. This nerdy scientist in a corduroy jacket talked about how we're all made of these elements that started out in stars and galaxies, so it's like humans are made from old parts of the stars, even stars really, really far away. It got me thinking about how it just makes sense to crouch down like that and howl at the moon and the stars, and for that matter, the sun. But when I tried to let out a little howl at the rosy dawn, it just didn't sound the same, sort of weak and puppy-like in the cold, misty air. That's when Maddy laughed a little, leaned over and kissed me on the lips.

The tattoo on her ass made sense to me then, and it made sense why I had to be good to see it. Chartreuse told me it was my weird, like a totem or a sign from fate or something, just like it was hers and Maddy's. Only I didn't need a dog boy to show it to me, because I had them.

When I got home at eight in the morning, Mom was waiting at the kitchen table, wearing her fuzzy pink housecoat, her hair up in curlers and that white stuff caked on her face. I didn't even get through the screen door before she stood up and started screaming at me. "I tried to make you into something! I got you a job and this is the thanks I get! I didn't want you whoring around town with every Tom, Dick and Harry!" Mom was screaming, sobbing, choking, shaking her head, sending big globs of cold cream glorping down onto the kitchen floor to form a pool like toxic waste. Fifi stood under her, looking frightened; a big glob of cold cream hit him on top of his head, and he ran off yelping. I just stood there on the front porch and looked at her like she was a complete freak. My

Dad appeared behind her in his underwear, those ugly boxer shorts Mom got him for Valentine's Day when I was a little kid. "I won't have it!" she howled again at the top of her lungs. The neighbors were starting to look out their windows.

"Uh...hi Mom," I said nervously, trying my best to sound friendly, even though I was convinced she had totally flipped. "It was actually Maddy and Chartreuse, you know, the girls I work with. I don't know anyone named Dick..."

Mom was weeping uncontrollably. She finally screamed and ran into the bathroom and locked herself in. That kind of wailing, like those songs whales sing, made the walls shudder.

Dad looked at me and shrugged, this lascivious smile on his face. "Was it fun?"

I looked back at him. "Was what fun?"

"Never mind," he sighed. Mom stayed in the bathroom all morning, sobbing and wailing, which was kind of a bummer because after that big Tom Collins I really had to take a whiz.

Mom and I didn't speak for a long time. She had really just misunderstood the whole thing and refused to apologize for the scene she'd made. I got back at her by lounging around the house all day in my underwear, and going out at night with Maddy and Chartreuse after work. Some nights, we would go out to the clearing to sit and just kind of hang out. Other times, we would do what we'd done the first night. Maddy told me they were really happy to have me along. I told her I was really happy to be there. But I knew I had to be leaving soon, the summer was almost over.

In September, I packed up my old suitcase with blue jeans and T-shirts and all the books Maddy had loaned me, and Mom and Dad drove me down to the Greyhound station. I was sad to be leaving Maddy and Chartreuse, but Mom and I still weren't talking much. She gave me a stiff, forced kind of hug and left a smear of orange lipstick across my cheek. "You keep your nose out of trouble, young lady," Mom said tightly. "I will, Mom." Then Dad hugged me and whispered, "Don't listen to her, Virginia," and winked. Mom overheard him, and shot him this look that might have killed a lesser man.

College *is* a lot cooler this year, even though Butch, of course, keeps hassling me for a date. *Puh-leeze.* Like I don't have better things to do with my time. I've got books to read; I promised Chartreuse I'd at least be done with *Macho Sluts* and *The Moon Goddess* so she can have them back when she comes here for Halloween. They're gonna take some time off, now that Maddy's in charge.

See, Maddy got a loan from this freaky old aunt of hers and bought Freddy out, so he retired to the next county over. Maddy tells me I'm not even going to recognize the place when she's done with it. She's calling the place Ginny's. I'm touched. She tells me they've built a skylight that lets them see the night sky, and a new sound system—from now on, Maddy says, no more of that Frank Sinatra stuff; it's Patsy Cline and Patti Smith, Elvis and Social Distortion and Richard Hell and the Voidoids all the way. She tells me word's getting around that things are changing for the better at Ginny's, and the old crowd has found other places to hang out. The new customers are people who can appreciate the power of the night the way Maddy and Chartreuse can. There's apparently this big crowd of lady truck drivers there every Friday for All-Patsy Night and one-dollar moonshine. And Maddy tells me a different kind of biker comes to Ginny's nowadays, guys from the next county over who come in two to a Harley. Maddy's even fixing up the back room.

The Change

Barbara J. Ferrenz

Rolling over onto her side, Karen awoke, a spear of sunlight striking her in the eye. She threw her hands to her face, then pulled them away as tiny grains sprinkled her cheek. She blinked her eyes to clear them. Her fingers were caked with sand. She clapped her palms together and watched as some fell off. Underneath the sand there was a sticky substance—dark and sticky. Tucking her chin into her chest to view the rest of her nude body, Karen saw similar patches of sand adhering to her breasts and stomach looking like candy rolled in brown sugar.

I saw something move over there. Call the kids in, will ya?

She covered her ears against the voices, forgetting the sand and the nasty stickiness. She knew the voices had nothing to do with her ears, that they were speaking deep within her brain and speaking only to her. She squeezed her head and hummed, rocking back and forth on her buttocks until the voices had gone.

Opening her eyes, she crawled into the sunlight and scanned the beach. Finding it empty, she gathered up her clothes and walked to the ocean's edge. There she bathed away the filth from the night before, letting the surf wash away her fears. She dressed, putting on the clothes she found crumpled beneath her each morning. Brushing away as much of the sand and as many of the wrinkles as she could, she mounted the wooden steps of the boardwalk. As the morning wore on and the beach goers came out, Karen began to blend in.

She had been on the beach for a week, but after only a couple of days she had every foot of the mile-long boardwalk memorized. She would walk up to the ocean lookout on one end, and then down a mile where the wooden planks ended suddenly on a dirty beach, where the rides, video arcades, and boom boxes were just a distant noise on the wind. The sea grass had grown tall here, the beach eroded and strewn with the decaying carcasses vomited from the sea. She had found a spot under the walk where she could spend her nights in relative peace. Beyond a drug deal and an amorous liaison between two underage kids, she had the place to herself.

She strolled past shops selling the same T-shirts, the same sunglasses, and the same buckets and shovels. The afternoon heat baked the sun lotion smell into a strong, heady perfume. Nearly naked people jostled by her throughout the day, not seeing the forty-something woman in the simple cotton dress with sandals. She felt almost content with the anonymity, the warmth, and the constant roaring surf drowning the whispers. In eight to ten weeks, the summer would be over and the chemicals in her body would have dissipated to nothing. Eight to ten weeks, and she would be free.

"It's just an anti-depressant, Karen. Hundreds...no, thousands of people take it with no ill effect."

"Then how do you explain these changes? Tell me, Doctor, why am I acting like this?" With the tears had come anger, tripping off an image in her head—torn sinuous meat, red and salty, hot and dripping. Karen salivated and took a Kleenex from her purse to dab the corners of her mouth. She felt warm and the sound of the doctor's voice hurt her head, like fingernails scraping against her skull. He touched her hand, and she drew it back. The curly, gray hairs on his wrist disgusted her. She wanted to rub his scent off her skin. She twisted the Kleenex into a tight noose.

"Karen," he said softly, oblivious to the pain he was causing her. "Given your age, we have to start thinking of the possibility of..." He smiled condescendingly, pipe smoke coiling from the corners of his mouth, "...menopause."

Karen sputtered, saliva spraying from her mouth as she tried to speak. Frustrating moments like this, when speech eluded her, were part of the problem. Up until a few weeks before, she had been a competent, tenured professor of sociology trying to cope with the anxiety of producing original, publishable research while teaching both gifted students and boneheads. She had become depressed about her non-existent social life since her divorce three years earlier. Within thirty minutes of entering Dr. Costanza's office for the first time, she had a prescription in her hands.

"Safe as aspirin," he had told her. Three weeks later, she needed a medical leave of absence from the university. Two weeks after that, she had been jailed for assaulting a young woman she didn't even know. She found it just as scary that she didn't know how she'd gotten to the part of the city where the attack had taken place. Dr. Costanza chewed on his pipe, looking at her with pity.

"I know this is hard for you," he said, "but the change is more difficult for some women than for others. Every person has a unique brain chemistry. You don't know what you'll set off when the balance is upset. Listen, Karen, I'm leaving on vacation this weekend, but I can prescribe..."

"No!" she barked. Karen forced her mind and voice to work together. The urge to hurt him—not with a weapon, but with her own hands and teeth—was overwhelming. She fought to subjugate those feelings to words.

"No more drugs! I'm not going to take any more! I hurt people! I have blackouts! I dream of blood! What have you done to me?"

"Nothing, Karen. I want to help you. Nobody is going to make you take the anti-depressant. Keep in mind that it will remain in your system for eight to ten weeks after you stop taking it, but menopause commonly..."

Karen stood up and walked to the door.

"It's not menopause. You fucked with my brain."

The music from the boardwalk carnival sounded eerie from a distance; the neon lights were a multicolor sunrise on the night sky. Jocelyn lifted her hair off of her neck and let the ocean breeze refresh her. She had gotten an uncomfortable sunburn and felt as if she had brought the heat of high noon into evening.

"What's down there? It smells bad."

"I'll tell you what's down here. No cops. I got some prime weed, and we're going to smoke it in peace." Randy mimed a long toke, ending with a spacey, satisfied grin.

Amanda dug her fists into the pockets of her windbreaker.

"Rest in peace is more like it. I don't know how you talked us into coming down here. It's dark and there's nobody else here."

"Go back then, wuss. Jocelyn and I will have a good time. Right, Joss?" Jocelyn smiled nervously and turned to the ocean. She didn't look forward to another evening of Mandy and Randy, the bickering twins. She had come to the beach with their family as company for Amanda, but found herself tagging along like a little-noticed pet.

"What's wrong with you?" Amanda asked in a strained voice, holding smoke in her lungs.

"Nothing. I just don't feel like smoking tonight." Jocelyn stood, tugging at her shorts and sweeping the sand from the backs of her legs. "I'm going down to the water."

Cooling her feet in the black waves made the sunburn more bearable. The rolling water sounded like a large crowd all talking at the same time, no one understanding what anyone else was saying. Feeling exposed, Jocelyn turned back to the twins. She saw their shapes still hunched on the beach.

From the corner of her eye, she thought she saw movement to her left. Facing that direction, she squinted at what could have been driftwood or a discarded bag of trash. She stood very still. A few moments later, she saw the dark figure get up on four legs and move rapidly toward the twins, crouching down again three yards away. They passed the pot back and forth, a sweet gray cloud forming over their heads.

Jocelyn took a step toward them. She thought to yell, but terror paralyzed her throat. She imagined that fleet-footed dark shape turning to her, chasing her into the ocean, trapping her. Tears ran down her face as she watched it stand once more and charge her unsuspecting friends.

She heard someone scream "No!" and hoarse cries, but otherwise, the kill was silent. Jocelyn stepped forward and back half a dozen times wanting to help, but not wanting to place herself in danger. A black, rolling mass on the sand...what could have been an arm...what could have been a tail.... It was over in minutes. The creature sank its teeth into Amanda's neck, moonlight glinting on her bangle earrings, and dragged her away through the sand. As it disappeared under the boardwalk, Jocelyn ran frantically up the beach in the direction of the neon lights.

Karen sat on the bench outside Thrasher's French Fries and wondered why she wasn't hungry. She had found herself here at the shore with no money, yet she had no need to buy food.

I got some prime weed, and we're going to smoke it in peace.
Rest in peace is more like it, Randy.

Aching cavern. Night hiding. Stark smell of food. Pulsing blood. Hungry. Crouch and wait.

Breaking into a fit of shakes, Karen stumbled down the boardwalk steps, reaching the cool dark beneath as her stomach heaved. Her mouth stretched wide and her gut fired its contents onto the sand, leaving her shivering and sweating. She held onto the thick, round piling for balance as she surveyed what had come out of her: a steaming pile of red, mucousy blood and chunks of semi-digested meat. The raw smell revolted her...and excited her. Her eyes widened as a wild thrill ran through her.

"Are you okay, ma'am?" A man stood in the sun a few feet behind her. *Stop the prey. Bite the throat. Don't let go.*

Karen waved her arms helplessly and shook her head. She felt trapped by this man. Her instincts commanded her to attack. She moaned as she searched for words to help her. A word came.

"Water."

"Sure, I'll get you a drink." He smiled and tried to take her arm. She jerked her elbow away. Back on the boardwalk, she fell heavily onto the bench. The man came back from Thrasher's with a tall paper cup of iced water.

"Maybe you should get a hat," he said. She drained the cup and crunched the ice between her teeth. She was feeling better.

"I beg your pardon?"

"A hat. I see you out here in the sun every day. Maybe it finally caught up with you. Too much sun can really do you in.

"Yes, thank you. A hat." *A hat on her head to hold in her brain.* The man was overdressed for the beach. Long pants and a sport coat, socks and shoes. He became serious. "I don't mean to scare you, ma'am, but you've been spending a lot of time around here by yourself."

"Is there a law against that?" Karen's face flushed with anger.

"Oh, no. Gosh, no. I'm just concerned, that's all. Haven't you read the paper? A couple of tourists have turned up missing. We even have a report of some kind of wild animal on the south beach."

"We?"

"Huh? Oh, yeah, we. The sheriff's department. I'm Sheriff Duncan. Phil Duncan. What's your name?"

What is my name? I haven't heard it in days.

"Susan."

Waking on her nest of clothes, she stands and stretches. She sniffs the bundle of cloth, knowing where she'll return to sleep after the hunt. The moon is high. The breeze off the water carries few familiar odors. She steps slowly to the edge of the deep shadows, peering out. Nothing moves but the water, which is crashing and retreating on the shore.

She moves quickly between the stanchions of the boardwalk without fear. Her gray coat is camouflage at night; she fades into the shadows. A sharp stab in her stomach hastens her step. The food she had buried under the sand is gone. Her reawakened hunger makes her bold and she crosses the open sand on her belly, her legs fold beneath her. She returns to the place of her last kill and sniffs. All signs have been washed away by the rising tide.

Returning to cover, she lopes further up the beach, closer to the light and noise but not close enough to reveal herself. The last kill had been easy. The prey came to her, outside her den. Tonight she will find a place to hide in wait. She snuffles the ground. Her hollow belly gurgles. Their scents are strong here. They will return.

She is alert and her eyes dart up the shoreline to the figure at the edge of the water. It has broken away from its pack and is moving along slowly, a stinking cloud rising from its head. It does not look her way. It is not wary of its surroundings. As it moves abreast of her, she can smell that it is male.

Slowly she gets to her feet, saliva dripping from her jaws. She dashes across the sand, her paws soundless. She stops and crouches, watching. She checks behind her and up and down the beach. The prey is moving farther away from the others. She lets it go. It is old and fat and slow, but it might cry out. She runs, keeping pace with it.

It is time. *Stop the prey. Bite its throat. Don't let go.* The muscles in her haunches tighten. Her heart beats faster with the smell of blood. She draws back, then propels herself forward across the beach, the wind blowing in her fur. A small distance away, she leaps, soaring, then lands heavily on the prey's chest, throwing it back onto the sand with a quiet *whumph*. Her jaws open, drool spinning onto the open neck. An odor fills her nose, human but confusing.

Karen...I want to help you...the change is more difficult for some women.... You don't know what you'll set off when the balance is upset.

The sound in her head enrages her, though she doesn't understand its meaning. It is familiar, yet threatening. The prey has squirmed out from under her. It stands and begins to lumber away, shouting. Returning calls echo down the beach. She should run away to protect herself, but she is compelled to silence the voice in her head.

You fucked with my brain.

Driven by a frenzy to destroy, she chases the prey and catches up easily. Sinking her fangs into the back of one leg, she rips the muscle and he falls. The blood flowing over her lips intoxicates her. She bites again and again, shredding flesh, setting loose the blood that fills her head, drowning the voices in a thick red sea.

He swings his bare arms and legs and she snaps at them. Pinching some skin in her teeth, she pulls, shaking her head and peeling the skin tufted with gray hair away from the shiny muscle beneath it. Growling, she jumps on his chest and looks into his white terror-stricken eyes. Her foot slips in the blood and she is face to face with him. She knows him. She knows the enemy. Her lips curl back from her gums. The salt air dries her teeth and a low snarl rumbles in her chest. That face. She hooks her top teeth into his brow, the bottom onto his jaw and digs and pulls, scraping bone. The face is sliced and shredded into wet, red strips. His screams turn to whines and then stop. He jerks in a final spasm.

Panting heavily, she steps away from the corpse exhausted, with no desire to feed, nor to drag it away to be buried. She is startled by the sudden presence of many humans, screaming and flashing painful lights. She turns in circles, trying to find an escape. Disoriented, she runs into one. He shouts in fear.

Maybe you should get a hat.

The familiarity of his sound and scent confuses her further. She remembers cool water on a parched mouth. She crouches in front of him in submission. He steps back and points a long metal rod at her. He lifts it to his shoulder. It smells burnt and oily. Sensing danger in his eyes, she bolts.

Explosions erupt around her, sending excruciating pain into her ears as she flees across the sand. Footsteps follow but are soon left behind in the dark. She will abandon her den and find a new hunting ground, a place to feed until the last of summer brings her home.

Euphorbia Helioscopia*

Jeremy E. Johnson

I never meant to get involved with anyone when I ran from the city to the lakeside cabin my father had built. Quite the opposite really. What with Matthew's cheating and laughable tear-wracked confession, followed swiftly by my throwing him out of our apartment, the last subject on my mind was sex. Or love.

We were married a year, not counting the two years spent living together beforehand, just to "test the water." Lukewarm water, it turned out. He couldn't keep his hands—among other parts of his body—off the waitress at his usual bar. So we divorced. When the papers came through in October, I moved out of the sterile, stuccoed complex with an inappropriately cheery name and drove my Honda eleven hours straight, with three stops for gas and coffee loaded with cream and sugar, to the family summer home in Michigan's Upper Peninsula.

Mom and Dad had been dead almost a decade. I don't really understand what compelled me to head north in October, but once I got there, the point was moot. November first, the day after a Halloween without trick-or-treaters, snow fell steadily from dawn until dusk. The Honda was buried up to the door handles. Luckily, I had stocked the pantry when I first arrived: another valuable lesson from Mom.

I didn't eat much anyway. I fed on my thoughts instead. Every morning, I got up whenever the sun told me to, lit the stove and put coffee on. Then I'd bundle up, take my mug outdoors, and alternate sipping the black brew and chipping firewood. Dad had believed in the power of fire: for cooking, heat and light. The woods surrounding our place provided plenty of fuel, as well as a cathedral for the

* Latin for the Wolf's Milk plant genus

mind. After my chores, just as my father had done, I took a fresh cup of coffee into the forest and wandered while I thought.

Thought. It's amazing where thought can take you. You can't think in the city: too many people, too much noise. Not unless you lock yourself away in a dark room and refute the world, hide away, deny everything. Out here, the pale blue, wispy sky...the skeletal, hibernating treetops...wind squalls groaning in forlorn anticipation of the next blizzard...squirrels skittering atop the icy, thin-skinned snow drifts...and your own boots sifting through the cold powder, crunching the dead leaves and twigs of fall's forgotten bottom layer...all this contributes to mental spelunking, encourages it. Each thump of your healthy heart, each deep-drawn and ice-prickled breath, the exhalation of smoke-warm cloudbursts hanging frozen in space until your stride carries you through it, breaking up the visible evidence of the life inside—all of it forms an arc of the spiraling cycle downward into Self.

I thought about a lot of stuff: the ex and whether I had made the right decision leaving him; Mom and Dad; even about kids. The ex never wanted children, and I went along, not willing to spoil the still wading pool of our relationship, fascinated by the drowning image of our stagnant lives under the algae. But out here in the beautiful wilderness, with the ghostly echoes of my childhood reverberating all around, my loneliness throbbed. I wished for a baby.

On the day I was meditating upon a name for this non-existent child, I found her.

I had been walking around the lake, getting further and further away from home, marveling at the frosty, sparkling whiteness of Mother Nature, thinking, at least here, she's still a virgin. Then I heard a startling cry ring out ahead, a combination of owl screech and fox yelp. I wondered what beast would make such a sound. Although it was an hour before noon and unusually sunny, I felt a twinge of fright.

When I had gone another few yards, I caught sight of her lying by the lake shore. From my distance, I could tell that she was completely naked. My first inclination was to rush to the aid of a fellow human being, but something held me back...an instinctive, trembling tentativeness that made me ashamed and cautious at the same time.

I edged forward, trying to make as little noise as possible, peeking from behind trees as I got closer. I've never been very graceful, however. Somehow, my foot managed to find the driest, most brittle, and loudest dead branch to step on. The young girl (I could tell she wasn't much older than sixteen or seventeen now) looked my way. I stood motionless, caught between two skinny white pines, exposed.

For a long moment, we simply stared at one another. I gazed, fascinated, into the most beautiful blue-gray eyes I had ever seen. Gypsy eyes, I thought. I still do. Her look never wavered, as if she were sizing me up. Why, I didn't know, but I instinctively trembled before her obviously steel-hard will like a sheep suddenly confronted by the dark and mythical wolf.

Then the tension broke. Her hand stretched toward me, begging, as another weird shriek came out of her mouth. Without thinking, I walked closer and saw why she remained at the shoreline.

Furriers and trappers from southern Michigan use this area to hunt small game. They come up for a weekend, scout out the wooded areas for tracks, then set traps for unwary animals. Some use the old-fashioned wire snares, rigged to trees and baited with sweetly poisoned foodstuffs. Others prefer a live capture, investing in tough metal cages. Most, however, stick to a cheap and effective method: steel jaws. They pry the spiked teeth apart, set the trigger plate, and cover the contraption under a thin layer of compost. When the creature steps on the broad paddle like an iron uvula at the jaws' center—
SNAP!

It doesn't care what part of the animal it clamps down on, just as long as it holds on tight, even if it's a naked teenaged girl's left foot.

I had gone close enough to see the hurt and pleading in her powerful eyes. In seconds and without thinking, I had freed her leg, wrapped my feather-stuffed winter parka around her shivering, blue-tinted body, and hustled her back toward the cabin. I tried to get the image of her hot, red blood staining the white, snowy ground out of my mind. And that steely, smeared grin lying there, faceless and triumphant.

Through it all, she never said a word.

On the way back to the house, the same questions kept running through my mind: Who was this young woman? Why was she naked? How had she come to the lake, to me? Nothing except the stereotype of the runaway answered my confusion. At the time, worried about her injury, I dumbly accepted this naïve supposition. Instead of grilling her about her identity, I laid her on my bed and fetched soap and water.

She bared her teeth at me when I first touched the wounded foot. Gleaming white ivory canines flashed between pale pink lips pulled back from the gums. A growl bubbled up from her throat, and a blood moon's coldness flared in her eyes. As I continued to cleanse the gashes, whispering soothing nonsense as I might do for a child of four, she relaxed enough to watch my ministrations almost curiously, occasionally giving a warning snarl when I pained her more than the wound, which still looked quite bad. I was convinced that the trap had bitten to the bone. Blood leaked out steadily so that by the time I had wrapped her leg, the stain spread visibly, a widening crimson circle on the innocent white bandages. If it looked worse in the morning, I'd have to drive her to the nearest town, even though I knew the Honda wouldn't make it to the end of the quarter-mile, drift-covered driveway.

Still, she neither spoke nor cried.

As I put away the first-aid kit my mother always made sure was well-equipped for any emergency, the girl blinked sleepily at me and gave a great, whining yawn. Then she formed a half-fetus, falling immediately into an afternoon drowse. I could tell it wasn't deep because her breathing came fast, almost panting.

She slept lightly until dark. I had slipped into my favorite flannel nightshirt, started a fire, and began cooking when I heard her sit up. Two shiny copper eyes reflected the flames, watching.

"What's your name?" I asked while offering her a mug of tomato soup. In reply, she licked my hand and nuzzled into my soft stomach. I didn't know whether to laugh or drop the food. God help me, my first inclination was to pet her head. I thought the blond tresses would have been more tangled than a bramble patch, but they were straight and coarse and smelled of the pines.

"What is your name," I murmured, no longer a question because she no longer nosed my belly button...she was lower, all warm breath and gentle intention. "What is your name," I chanted on, stroking her head until the soup lost its importance. I tossed it on the floor and buried both hands deep in her forest-scented hair instead. The mingling of hot, spilled tomatoes and cool green pine excited me. I don't know why. Maybe it was the thought of the city so far away and no one here to tell me what I was doing was wrong, immoral.

I lifted off my nightshirt, dropped it on the floor to sop up the soup, and threw myself at the nameless girl whom I had saved. She returned the passion with equal measure, scampering across my body as if it were an open field, nipping playfully, with just the right amount of tongue and teeth. More delirious than confused, I followed suit. I plied her pale skin, pinched until it turned from pink to red and she sighed. Her taste danced on my lips like a falling crystalline stream.

We were animals.

It had been an extraordinarily long time since my last sexual encounter. That's the only explanation I had for my overpowering desire. I'd never been with a woman before either, but I didn't have time to mull over these troubling thoughts. When I awoke the next morning, the girl was gone.

Immediately, a familiar sinking feeling sucked at the center of my chest and I knew I had ventured into dangerous territory. Sex—and love—might have been the last things on my mind, but now they were part of an irresistible, unavoidable reality.

I got dressed and went out to search for her. My greatest fear was finding her frozen on the bottom porch step or back in the jaws of another man-trap. Looking around, I managed to discover half-effaced tracks leading east: she was traveling on all fours. Because I still didn't know her name, I periodically stopped along the trail to yell randomly. After two miles, the trail disappeared completely, erased by wind and a bout of fresh-fallen snow, so I headed back to the house.

Five dead rabbits lay on the porch, just outside the half-open door. Their necks had been snapped cleanly, glazed brown eyes staring up at me in surprise. Despite my earlier vexation at her disappearance, and my even deeper resentment at my own growing attachment to this free spirit, I swept indoors and found her waiting in bed for me, just where I'd hoped she'd be. Her mouth tasted of fur and meat and the hunt. I gulped her breath as though it were dandelion wine.

We ate rabbits for dinner.

I stewed three, after cleaning them thoroughly, while she kept two outside. The snapping of tiny bones resounded painfully in the crisp evening air. Strangely, hearing her guttural feasting made me hungry; the overcooked stew didn't satisfy. I sipped and watched her out on the porch, cleaning up, licking her hands and running them through hair turned silver in the moonlight. When she came in, her face shone pink and healthy, and I was jealous.

That's how things went for a couple of weeks. I never did find out her name because she couldn't—or chose not to—speak. It didn't matter. I, too, lost the use for words as we communicated through grunts and barks, nips of teeth and playful slaps. Our eyes spoke the most.

I changed the bandage on her leg once. After peeling off the stiffened, burgundy-stained original wrap, I realized her recuperative powers transcended most other humans'. The gashes resembled purple puckers well on their way to being healed. No more blood. I dressed them again just to keep dirt out of the knitting scars, but she had torn it off by the next day. I found her by the log pile in a contortionist's pose, licking the wound clean, and I ceased to worry about the injury that had brought us together.

My appetite changed. She continued to hunt for us, bringing home more rabbits, pheasant, and once, a fawn. The deer meat tantalized when she dragged the barely mauled carcass onto the porch. I had spent an hour preparing a heavily seasoned broth, stoking the fire in anticipation of her kill, but when I saw the trophy, I felt compelled to celebrate in her style. Together we consumed the dead animal. That was the best meal I'd ever had.

Man discovered fire, right? So women have no obligation to use it.

We spent a lot of time in bed, then on the rug before the cold hearth, and finally, outdoors. Even though winter had become crystalline and frigid, we greatly preferred being beneath the blue-black skies dotted with faraway stars squinting down at us and the swaying, rustling firs on every side while we nestled in the snow, miraculously untouched by frost, reveling only in each other's inner warmth.

If it hadn't been for the howls, we probably never would have returned to the house. She loped indoors when the first soul-ringing peals came down from the higher ground surrounding our valley. All I could do was follow, fearfully aware of my nakedness for the first time.

Three days passed, and the howling came closer every night. We shivered against each other, gnawing on whatever rations I had in the pantry that needn't be cooked. Confusion clouded my eyes; she stared back at me with an awful knowledge. Whatever was coming, she knew it…and it knew her.

At dusk last night, the front door flew open and a shadow-cloaked figure stood on the threshold. My wild, instinctive dislike for this intruder took over and I flew to the attack, all teeth and snarling violence. A dark hand swatted, effortlessly sprawling me halfway across the room. In that moment before my cursory dismissal, I could see the trespasser. She stood outlined by the doorframe, with the moon shining white from behind. At first, I thought she remained in a perpetual shadow, until I realized her unclothed body was the shadow. Her skin had the bruised cast of an early morning thundercloud. Beneath the midnight-inked flesh, wiry muscles vibrated and sharp bones protruded. Her eyes, like polished steel marbles, stared unblinking into mine. Dark waves of regal pride emanated from her stance.

Stunned, I watched as the woman called the girl to her side as she might a faithful hunting dog who had strayed. There was a pause as the girl made to bite the exposed fingers, then snuffling the woman's scent, licked her palm instead.

She had recognized her mistress.

I felt the old jealousy rise inside, and a cold protective urge that was anything but motherly. An unbidden growl escaped my lips. The woman howled ferociously in reply. My eardrums vibrated from the explosive reprisal as I shamefully groveled on the floor before this entity who now owned my lover, had probably always owned her. I became insignificant before this goddess of mountains and woods, felt her command of Nature and absolute rule over any who dwelled on this tiny patch of Earth. What could I have done?

So I watched, helpless, as the woman led my lover away. The girl looked longingly at me over her shoulder, a plea for forgiveness. She needn't have asked for it; I fully realized the tether by which she was tied. They disappeared into the night.

I yelped and yowled in my loneliness the rest of the evening until I became hoarse, finally falling asleep on the floor. When I awoke to the sun and an empty house, I began to follow them. I don't know where they've gone, although I've been able to track their scents so far, following them even further into the mountainous regions. Thankfully, my sense of smell has grown more acute in the past month. I imagine they're in a place of idyllic wilderness, a sheltered haven of romp and feast and escape, far from the city and far from man. The woman-goddess will have me, I know. She could have killed me last night, but spared me. She knew I would come to her, if only to be close to her pet. And she's right. I don't intend to live in a world without the girl.

I love her.

The Hound of God

Tom Piccirilli

She awoke huddled under a bed, her right hand throbbing, and the unraveled guts of a broken box spring and torn mattress above her, leaking out like a sheaf of cotton. The smell of pancakes and sausage swelled in the small, hot room. Someone limped past her field of vision: from this low vantage point, she saw the cuffs of ragged white trousers, brown socks with black slippers, the toes cut out to ease pressure on the bunions. Marcel. She hadn't realized his feet were getting so bad.

Tangera drew her aching hand up before her eyes and saw she'd been bandaged. Bits of dried flesh and blood clung to her fingernails. She unwound the soiled wrappings to find she'd been shot in the fleshy part of her palm with a small caliber bullet. Marcel and the others had become good at doctoring her wounds. She crawled out.

"Mornin', Ma'am," he said, bowing his bald head. He averted his eyes as he always did, not merely at her nudity, but in a deference she hated but would not deny him. A robe had been set out on the kitchen chair and she put it on. "'Spects you're hungry. Got your favorites cooking, be done in a minute. Don't be worrying none about the time. It ain't even seven yet, you ain't late for work. Don't worry."

"Who saw?"

He shrugged. "Everybody, I 'spect. Happened up on the roof. Pretty early too. Wasn't even midnight. Them boys was just itchin' for judgment day. Crackheads, a'course. Seems like they all crackheads nowadays. Don't see 'em much with guns though. I was kinda surprised at that. How's your hand?"

She flexed it. "Fine. Thanks for patching me up."

"I didn't do much, just helped Mama Sabelle."

A short gasp of apprehension hitched in her throat and her bad hand trembled slightly. She kept her voice level. "I don't know that name. Who is she?"

"Nice woman, moved in a few months ago. You got nothing to be a'fright of. She's from Jamaica. She understands these things better than most of Harlem."

His casualness made her anxiety worse, but there was nothing to be done at the moment. "You need to see a podiatrist. I know a good one on Forty-ninth."

"I hate downtown."

"So do I most of the time, but you're going. I'll make an appointment this afternoon."

"Okay. Here's your breakfast."

After eating, she went up to her apartment. Flowers and cans of vegetables and soup had been placed outside her door, along with the spoils of last night: two .45s and a pair of supreme pump, NBA performance, high-top sneakers valued at perhaps two hundred dollars. She picked up the guns—both clips empty—checked the size of the sneakers, took them too, and nudged the rest of the tribute aside with her foot. In a few days, the others would gather and take the gifts away, but not until they were certain Tangera had had a chance to properly decline the offerings.

She showered at length and rebandaged her hand, brushed the grime and mattress stuffing out of her hair, and afforded herself a long look in the mirror. She had virtually the same body now as she did when she ran track at UCLA a decade ago, with no softening in the breasts or belly, not even at the point of her chin where her mother had first started to age. She dressed, grabbed a copy of James Baldwin's *Another Country* from her nightstand and threw it in her briefcase. On the way to the station, she dropped the guns into the mailbox on the corner, where Arthur the mailman would dispose of them. She made the subway with no time to spare and read the entire ride down to Wall Street.

At lunch, recent college grad but already ascending star in the firm, Freddy Hennison, hit on her again, throwing everything he'd learned about co-eds into the attempt. He'd already mowed through four of the fifteen ladies in the office, especially attracting the married women. Tangera had watched in subdued fascination as he made his rounds over the past six months, starting at the west end of the room and working east, hoping he was just a bit too white bread to chase after a black woman. Even some of the more aggressive ones got scared off by the interracial scene, but the past couple of weeks had proven Freddy Hennison otherwise.

He leaned against her desk and struck a pose like an Art 101 nude model, so that she got the full view of his biceps, hips, the fine line of his jacket, the jutted cup of his groin—fairly impressive. He bled boyish charm. "You've hurt yourself."

"I'm all right," she said.

And that was the end of his concern, the opening volley already initiating friendly conversation. She could see pride in his eyes. "How about you and I spend a quiet afternoon at A Taste of Paris, Tangie?" he asked. The diminutive of her name made her cringe. "I've already made reservations and they serve the finest chicken cordon bleu in the city. Trust me. You like French?"

He must have made the reservations already, thinking about her all this time, stewing in his own juices. Tangera grinned at him, trying to keep the mood light, although she knew it would swing soon enough, understanding what would happen but unable to stop it. When men got this desperate so early in the game, things could only turn ugly. He'd been planning too far ahead. "That's very considerate, Freddy, but I'm afraid I've got to work through lunch."

He had a nice smile, no warmth to it, but no smarminess either, only a generous sense of appeal. "How about tonight then? We can take in a show, maybe go dancing at *Moulin Rouge*. You put in way too much overtime. You need to learn how to relax. Take me for instance. I know how to savor life." He flashed his dimples in a way that seemed natural enough; he must have worked on that one for a while.

"I need the money," she said.

"Tangera, when are you finally going to realize you're as infatuated with me as I am madly in love with you?"

"You're overplaying it, Freddy. I nearly broke at the sight of those dimples, but now you're looking for the Academy Award. Sorry."

His tone downshifted to just this side of rude. He was still playing it fairly loose, but with a few barbs now. No one else in the office was around, no other audience to play up to besides his ego. "Why do you live in that dump uptown?"

For the first time, Tangera smiled. "How do you know where I live?"

He chuckled without humor, slinging his jacket over his other arm, cutting off the view of his groin as if punishing her. "Ah, I must

admit I was a little curious about you and checked Personnel."
Freddy had a way of leaning in on women as he spoke, forcing them
to either feel his breath on their flesh or withdraw a step and get
wedged into the corner. "There's an opening in my building. You'd
love the place, I'm telling you."

"I like where I live."

"In Harlem, for Christ's sake? I thought you people worked hard
to get out of places like that."

Suddenly, the migraine blazed to life, sizzling very particularly
into her temples. Freddy's face seemed momentarily replaced by
another, and then another, features writhing and re-forming into
others she had known but barely remembered, all the way back to
her father. A soft, repetitive sound grew stronger, much louder, until
the pounding filled her mind. She recalled her mother's calming
touch and wished for it now—the compresses on her forehead, the
teas that fought the fevers. Tangera ran her tongue over her teeth.
That familiar taste flooded her throat.

She realized the sound was the clicking of her fingernails against
the desk.

He reached out to smooth his fist over her arm, making for the
lean, pressing in and closing off her space. She drew away and his
hand grabbed her gently, but firmly. Her mother's voice slithered
into her ears, the rhythmic Nigerian accent like lovely music, telling
her again that this was the land of opportunity; in this country you
could do, and be, anything if you were only willing to work for it.
Tangera tried to keep herself from hyperventilating. "You've still got
a lot of other women in this place to try for, Freddy, and at least half
of those left are married. Why not just call this one a wash and leave
me alone?"

"Tangera, listen, what's...?"

He grasped her more tightly now, tugging. His sweet smile had
melted into something not quite a sneer but heading in that direction. Her mouth eased open into a wide grin. "Take your goddamn
hand off me, Freddy."

"You high yellow bitch. Who in the hell do you think you are?"

"Oh, now there's a question," she said and burst out laughing
into his face, and those of all the other men, including her father's.
Her nostrils flared, the smell of his desire and rancor so palpable it

made her dizzy. Her fingernails abruptly quit, the sound and the migraine draining from her head until the clarity of this moment was so intense and pure that she groaned. Her breath came in quick, little gasps. Freddy backed away with a look of disgust.

In a moment she was on him, vaulting the desk and taking him down in one fluid motion, her hand covering his mouth, and her teeth instantly at his neck. Another millimeter and her canines would snap through the soft cartilage of his trachea. His muffled shouts were in sync with her screaming pulse. "Maybe I will move, Freddy," she whispered. "You and I could have some fun, right? Yeah. So what's your address? Hey. Hey, are you listening? Are you savoring this, baby?"

She found herself on the subway at her stop, the bandage having unraveled and trailing beside her, *Another Country* opened to a page about two chapters further than she remembered reading.

Gunshots echoed across alleys as she made her way back to the building. She stood on the doorstep and heard shrieks and the not-too-distant whine of ricochets. She coughed as though the noises of her life were choking her.

A boy no more than eight was sifting through the offerings in front of her apartment door, carrying three cans of beets under an arm. Sweet perfume of dead flowers cloyed the hallway. He picked at and discarded Boston beans, clucking loudly, "Yech." When he saw her, he drew a wracked breath, eyes flitting in terror.

"You can take them," she said, but the boy hurriedly dropped all of the cans. Tangera bent and retrieved them, holding them out. "Really, here, let me give them to you."

"No, Ma'am. I'm sorry. I'se just..."

"Don't be. You like beets? Can't stand them myself. Do me a favor and take everything here, will you? Except the Boston beans. Those are my favorite. What's your name?"

He obviously considered lying, but was too unsure of the notion, expecting that to be caught in such a deception would be even worse. "David."

"Hello, David. I'm Tangera."

"I know." He studied her for a time and the atmosphere in the hallway took on a different element, the scent of rotting flowers almost too heavy to breathe in. She discovered with some surprise that she wanted to run but had no idea in which direction to move. Sirens blared and another gunshot popped. Finally he gathered his courage—just as she felt her own dwindle to nothing—and said in a nearly inaudible voice, packed with reverence, "My mama say you been kissed by de woof. Dat de woofs fight witches in hell, and if de witches close de door to hell we get no water and everybody's food dies."

"Who is your mother, David?"

"Mama Sabelle."

It was a tale she knew well—about how wolves served mankind and kept watch over the solstices as the hounds of God—but the superstition was European, and not even well-known there. How did a woman from Jamaica come by the myth?

"She's a kind woman. She helped me when I needed it."

"Your hand."

Tangera swallowed thickly. "Yes."

"I gots to go."

"All right. I hope to see you again."

She called the podiatrist's office only to find that she'd already made an appointment earlier in the day. After rereading the chapters in the Baldwin novel and watching the evening news, she brought the sneakers to Marcel. "Here, these ought to fit you."

He laughed until he wheezed. "Ooh, them the supreme pumps. Damn, they fine. Nice and big. Ain't gonna hurt my bunions none. Never had as nice a pair as these. Damn, them crackheads know how to live good when they ain't dead."

A knock at the door brought Marcel highstepping to answer it, strutting like he was ready to play ball now or run around Central Park. He opened the door and a humongous woman followed him inside carrying a tray of exotic meats and a bowl of stewed vegetables, nothing Tangera had ever seen before. She could smell the cooked beets, though. David huddled close to the woman, unsure of where to go or what to say, whether to show Tangera any greeting at all.

Marcel said, "Mama Sabelle, I want to introduce you to Tangera here."

Mama Sabelle averted her eyes as well, and David did the same. She made a series of subtle signs with her fingers, none of which Tangera knew. The woman had more than girth—Mama Sabelle virtually exuded power. She had seen and done a lot, and instead of bending her back, the weight of those years lined her body. She reminded Tangera of her mother, who had also been beautiful in her obesity until murdered in a movie theater by a fifteen-year-old girl, taking a bullet in the face meant for the teenager's cheating boyfriend who was sitting two rows in front. Years her mother had never seen, having died so young, and her father dying so damn late. That Nigerian music came into her head again, along with her father's belligerent grunts, and before long Tangera was weeping, kneeling before Mama Sabelle, her bandaged hand up before her in a gesture of need or protection, and she rocked there on the floor, helpless, repeating soundlessly, mama mama mama.

Mama Sabelle said simply, "The moon come risin', chil'."

Tides of dancers at the *Moulin Rouge* rolled in and out across the levels. She'd gone to see some nightlife for herself and join several women from the office. Freddy stared at her in lost puzzlement, wondering whether he should still be afraid. She could tell the day's events were already fading from his memory; that charm had nearly reignited once again. The man she danced with, Bradley Derry, as black as Stygia but with light red hair like Malcolm X, kept a fair distance from her, not attempting to grind his crotch into hers. She could smell only the faintest hint of liquor on his breath.

At two a.m., as if an alarm had gone off inside her, she stopped dancing and frowned, deciding halfheartedly to call it a night. "I'd like to see you again," Bradley said. "Will you give me your number?"

"Sure." He handed her a pen and billfold with a note pad in it, and she wrote down her name and number.

He glanced at the paper and said, "Where's your place?"

She told him and his smile widened, his eyes tinged with not quite the proper amount of fear. "You live in Harlem? I'd, uhm, better drive you home."

"Don't be ridiculous, it's all right."

"No, please, let me."

"I..."

"Come on, let's go."

Tangera waved to Freddy as they left and Freddy sucked down his gin and tonic in one dash. *I'll kill the bitch for thinking my white ass isn't good enough for her...if I can't have it from her then she ain't gonna give it away to some gorilla she met on the dance floor.* He thought about following them, but Tangera stared him down, letting him know that the little cue cards in his mind were large enough for her to see. She grinned as he rushed into the throng.

In the car, she and Bradley had an animated conversation. He walked with her to the building and didn't make any advances to get inside. He now had the look of someone who was mildly terrified but more interested than scared. She enjoyed watching black people who did not understand the other ways of the city. Bradley stared at the crackheads lying among the garbage cans, the brothers huddled on the corner cranking their gangsta rap even at this late hour. She drew the night in and saw him trying to do the same. They kissed briefly and made promises to see one another again.

She went to the roof.

The moon pulled her thoughts from her, drawing up all the threads of memory and nightmare.

I am Tangera: chocolate creamsicle, honey-mama bitch for all the black and white boys on the street to follow like dogs; for the men who offer roses, nights on Broadway, champagne-filled shoes, a handful of crack, the juice of a .45, a summer morning in Central Park on the lake; reckless, raunchy nights making love splashed up against the freezing window of a penthouse, naked and wet before the entire city; squatting out on the fire escape with marijuana and spray paint thick in the air; I am a lunatic, hysterical maniac, woman out of the sun; I am a Nubian princess, or some other named or nameless damned, the curse treading back to the black soil of the Nile, where my greatest-great grandfathers crossed the continent to mix majiks with the Khem of Egyptian priests of Thoth; I am daughter of Anubis, I am the hound of God.

She heard someone screaming.

Tangera awoke huddled under Marcel's bed, the guts of the broken mattress above her leaking out like a sheaf of cotton. Lying above her, David peered down, watching her with distinct amusement in his eyes, like staring at a pet, the sunlight shedding a red sheen over his face.

"I watched what you did last night from mah window."

"What?" she asked. "What did you see, David?"

He giggled, a sad and hideous sound. "Dem carjackers. You went right into de street after dem and hep that man. He kept screamin' and cussin', all cut up, until you got there. Then he drive away."

David retreated out of view, then handed down a knife. "Mama say dis yours now. Should I put it in fronta your door?" The blade was crusted with blood.

"No. Later you can go put it in the mailbox on the corner."

"Okay." And then later, much later, from above her, he asked, "Ma'am, can I be a woof, too?"

She waited. As if her tongue had the ages of lost African civilizations and American dreams instead of the pungent tang she could still taste on it, she gave him the same advice her murdered mother had given her as a child—honest but hollow, more truth than lie, but not the whole truth—she whispered, hoping he really wouldn't hear her, "You can be anything you want to be."

Visitation

Pamela J. Jessen

"And how are we this morning, Mrs. Cory?" the nurse asks as she sweeps through the door of my room. Her gaze never touches mine as she moves the curtains and checks the water level in the pitcher on the table beside my bed. She stirs a light wind with her rushing, a breeze laden with bitter medicinal smells, acrid antiseptic wipes and hurriedly washed bedpans. "Feeling up to visitors today?"

This nurse reminds me of a bird, with her quick, rapid movements. For a moment she seems to blur, then steadies again, peering sharply at me for the first time. Yes, quite, I decide, like a bird, hollow-boned and delicate. I imagine she would be easy to overcome, her bird bones shattering like fine china with the first blow. But I keep my hands in my lap, my claws safely sheathed. The nurse continues to gaze expectantly and I remember, vaguely, a question. She has asked me a question that evidently requires an answer. That is unusual. Most often the nurses' chatterings require little of me other than the occasional nod or grunt.

"What?" The sound of my voice is frightening, the barest whisper of my old, firm tone. It sounds quavery, worn-out, old. I clear my throat and try again. "What did you say?"

The nurse frowns, but it is a nice frown, full of concern, and I feel guilty for imagining her as a bird, as prey. "Your family called. They're coming to visit. If you're not up to it, we can cancel it."

My family! The pulse in my throat quickens, roars. "Of course I'm up to it," I say, and this time I've found my true voice. It's all I can do to keep my claws from springing out fully. My skin feels stretched and dry over my bones and I wish I could tear it all off and start fresh. *Change.* My fingertips itch from the effort of remaining sheathed. I run my tongue over my teeth, nicely sharp, just a hint pointed, not too noticeable unless I want them to be noticed. Unless I want to tear....

My family!

The nurse helps me to the bathroom. Gratefully she allows me the privacy I need for cleansing and bodily functions. When I emerge, damp and smelling of hospital soap, she helps me into comfortable baggy, dark blue slacks and a white blouse and sits me in the one comfortable chair in the room.

From here, I can see through my open door to Mrs. Hourigan's room. In my narrow field of vision is the end of her bed, a shelf with a vase of wilting flowers and her brush and comb. We visit on occasion, usually when the orderlies park us in wheelchairs in the hallway while our rooms are being scrubbed. I wonder if she is awake. Slowly, I stand and walk to her door. The orderlies make us use wheelchairs more for their convenience than ours.

"Mrs. Hourigan, are you awake?"

She lies in her bed, the covers pulled up as though she were suffering from a chill. Her head is turned away from me, and she does not answer. Sudden movement under the covers catches my eye, and something long and narrow snakes out at the side of the blanket, then vanishes again. A moan comes from the bed.

I stiffen, holding my breath for the moment it takes the image to resolve itself. An IV tube runs from her covered arm to a bag suspended beside her bed. She stirs again, and I am caught by a feeling of utter uselessness. Slowly, I return to my own room.

Soon, an orderly brings me a tray with juice, toast, prunes and Cream of Wheat. The toast is dry and cold and the Cream of Wheat is lumpy and made without salt or sugar so that the resultant gruel tastes more like library paste than cereal. What I wouldn't give for a cup of coffee—dark, rich, steaming hot, flavored with real cream and two sugars.

I sigh and begin to eat. The nurse returns and fusses a few minutes, smoothing the sheets of my bed, straightening the magazines on the bedside table, emptying the stale water from my water glass, refilling it, replacing the straw. In many ways, she is more maid than nurse. Her hair is light brown, pulled into a loose bun at the back of her head. A few strands have escaped this punishment and curl charmingly against her thin neck. Her nose is pointed, like the beak of a bird, and she is very thin. Too thin to make much of a meal, I decide, as I dip the corner of toast into the Cream of Wheat to soften it a bit. I may as well be eating cardboard, but the nurse will be disappointed if I don't eat at least a portion. She might think I am too ill for visitors, and my family is on its way.

But...who will come? I have been in this place—convalescing, I believe, is the term Dr. Sanchez uses, from an attack my traitor body has made on my mind—for quite some time. I can't recall exactly how long and sometimes that bothers me. But in all that time, my whole family—Charles, Louis and Roxanne—have gathered here only once and that was to bring me here and see me safely ensconced. Put away. Warehoused. Out of harm's way—or theirs. Away from Change.

I think of my children: Charles, so handsome, tall, white-blond hair and pale blue eyes, always so sure of himself; Louis, smaller and darker, more like me while Charles favors his father, Robert; then there is Roxanne, lovely with her long, pale hair, a feminine version of Charles and Robert. Would they bring their wives and husband? Their children? It would be like Christmas! I glance out the narrow window to be sure there is no snow on the ground, to be sure that a holiday is not the reason for this visit. But no, winter has not yet arrived. The maples and elms glow with autumn colors, drifts of golden leaves gathering on the lawn. Late October, I think.

My thoughts wander from the children to my husband, Robert, and my fingers itch again with unrealized fur and claws. I close my eyes and feel the wind on my face and taste the forest scent of him, the wildness of our passion, his teeth sharp against my neck. Our time before children seems brief now, tantalizing, unreal. Or more than real. I picture Robert, green eyes flashing in the moonlight as we change, chasing each other through the midnight woods surrounding our mountain cabin, the place we were most ourselves, free from prying eyes. The place, at last, where our children were born and other change inevitably set in.

I doze briefly. The orderly wakes me when he brings lunch. Today, there is a thin soup of greasy yellow chicken broth with a few pallid noodles floating in it, along with a square of bilious green gelatin, a raisin cookie and a carton of milk. For a moment, I close my eyes, picturing a steak leaking red juices onto my plate, inhaling imaginary aromas, but when I open my eyes there is only soup. The orderly is of medium height, lean, well-muscled, able to defend himself easily. I sigh and begin to eat.

After lunch I am restless. I pace up and down the hallway, from window to window. The nurses and orderlies glance at me from time to time and whisper to each other, gauging my mood. Mrs.

Hourigan's door is shut now. Eventually I tire and return to my room and my chair.

I try to read, but my mind wanders to Robert, to his leaving. He had been patient and gentle during my pregnancy, kind and attentive. But I could sense, also, an underlying unease that built in intensity over the course of time. The triplet birthing was hard, the early months of the children's lives a blur of feedings and tendings. Robert helped, but I knew he longed for the wildness of our other nights, the freedom of our moonlit runs. He began to go out alone, coming back exhausted at dawn when the children were beginning to stir. He spent long hours staring out the window. One night, he went out and never came back.

I stayed, raised the children, refusing for many years to think about that time with Robert. When the children would ask about their father, I would tell them he had been killed in an accident. Occasionally, I felt his presence in the woods nearby, as though he were waiting for something or someone. Perhaps me. Maybe one of the children. When that happened, I would close the windows, draw the curtains and turn the radio on very loudly, banishing him from my life once more. But lately I find myself looking out the window more and more, wondering about him, wondering if there is still some echo of my earlier self. I have not given in to the Change in all these years, although I feel it coiled within me, waiting. And Robert—does he still wait for me?

"Mrs. Cory?" The nurse again, her head poking around the door-jamb. "Are you awake? Your visitors are here."

"Of course." I blink, clear my throat. "Of course. Come in."

A tiny girl skips into the room, her white-blond hair pulled back in an elaborate braid, decorated with blue ribbons. A smile creases her round face and her green eyes remind me forcefully of Robert. She clutches a few stems of mums the color of frostbitten pumpkins in her chubby fist.

"Hi, Gramma!" She climbs nimbly into my lap and plants a sticky kiss on my cheek. "Do you like the flowers? Mama let me pick them myself."

I fold this flower of a child in my arms and return her kiss. She is warm against my breast and I can feel her energy flowing around us both, almost an embrace in itself.

"They're wonderful flowers, dear," I say, releasing her. "Where is your mother?"

"She's coming. Uncle Charles and Uncle Louis, too. They said I could come first 'cause they were talking to somebody."

"The doctor?"

She shrugs, sliding down from my lap. "Can I put the flowers in some water?"

Before I can respond, she has deposited the flowers in my water glass where they stand at comical angles, too tall for their container. I smile.

"Thank you, Deirdre."

"Hello, Mother," Roxanne says, coming into the room at last. Her hair is cut short, very practical, and she wears a long, dark blue sweater over cream-colored leggings. A few, tiny wrinkles have found their way to her forehead and around her mouth. "How are you feeling today?"

Before I can answer, Charles and Louis enter and greet me. Charles has put on weight, taking on a slightly swollen appearance, and his hair, once thick and long, has thinned and recedes from his high, pale forehead. Louis, though, is thinner than ever, and his dark eyes spark nervously as they dart from me to his siblings and niece. A warm noise surges through the room. I smile and offer my cheek to each one in turn, clasp hands, remark on how good it is to see everyone. They offer excuses for absent spouses, older children.

They settle eventually, like dust motes in sunlight. Charles and Roxanne sit on the edge of the bed, Louis leans against the door, while Deirdre, who is too young to settle, moves restlessly around the room, fingering books, other plants and flowers, counting the tiles on the floor. At last she spots the control for raising and lowering the bed and contents herself with that until her mother tells her to stop.

I watch my children and am amazed at their utter normalcy. Nowhere do I see a trace of Robert's wild energy or even of mine. They appear very much at home in their skins, content—whereas I still chafe at the limits imposed by my body. How is it that we have so little in common? In all the years I've spent caring for my children and now they for me, how is it that I have failed to share the most important part of myself? Have they felt the odd stirring under their skins, the urge to run through midnight woods, to rip and tear and roar their delight at a smoky moon?

Deirdre comes to me again, wrapping her arms about the arms of my chair. "Gramma, do you know what today is?"

I stroke her head, noting how the ribbons are plaited so intricately as to appear to grow with her hair. When Roxanne was small I'd never had the patience to do special things like this. And Roxanne had never wanted it. Or had she? Gradually, I become aware of an expectant hush in the room. A question. What has Deirdre asked? Do I know the day? Can it be her birthday? I cast through dates in my mind, discarding first one, then another.

"Gramma..." Impatience creeps into her voice.

"What day is it?"

If it is possible to smile with one's whole body, Deirdre does so. "It's Halloween! Mama says I can go trick-or-treating tonight."

Deirdre prattles on about Halloween, her costume, how much candy she expects, but my eyes are for Roxanne, for Charles, for Louis. Their smiles are for each other, for Deirdre. Roxanne glances at me and rubs her arms under her sweater. "The weather is lovely for this late in the year, isn't it Charles?"

"Oh, yes. I remember lots of Halloweens with snow on the ground."

"I love Halloween," I say, remembering other years, other whens, other Halloween rituals before Robert left. I do not speak of these to my children. To them, Halloween means trick-or-treat candy and silly costumes. I saw to that, as I see to their continuing ignorance of their true natures. Or, at least, of mine.

"Would you like to go outside for a bit, Mother?"

The nurse brings a wheelchair as if on cue, and we are going outside into the bright October air. How long has it been since I've been outside? The prospect is exciting; I feel my skin begin to stretch, my fingers flex and itch. They offer me a sweater, but I refuse. Louis drapes it over his arm in case I change my mind and we go out of the room, down the long hallway to an elevator, ride down two floors, down another hallway, through double doors and outside at last.

The air is flavored with a Halloween tang—decaying leaves and smoky pumpkins, apples and frost. Sun slants down between lowering clouds. They mill aimlessly around my wheelchair as if uncertain of what to do now. Deirdre hops over the cracks in the sidewalk, back and forth, back and forth. Charles lights a cigarette, coughs once. I frown my disapproval; he shrugs, takes a deep puff and turns away slightly.

"Let's walk," I say, pushing myself out of the wheelchair and taking a couple of steps toward the grassy lawn and wooded area beyond.

Louis and Roxanne hurry to each take an arm, but I wave them away. I'm feeling better than I have in a long while. The air and sunshine invigorate me and I feel as I did all those years ago when... .

I blink, take two steps away from Louis and Roxanne. There, at the edge of the trees, that flash of green eyes and pale blond hair. I rub at the skin of my arms, my face—the itch and stretch of dried out, too-tight flesh pulses in time to the pounding of my heart. Two steps more, away from my suddenly too-loud children and toward the green eyes waiting for me by the trees.

Wind sends dried leaves scurrying across the open spaces, carrying scents of forest and mountains beyond this place, of snow already whitening barren peaks. Behind me, Roxanne calls out to her daughter, "Don't go too far. Stay where I can see you." Charles smokes. Louis shifts from one foot to the other, watching Roxanne and Deirdre, Charles. Other flavors, other smells, tease my senses— the vanilla scent of pine, damp earth, the deep musky odor of loss. Robert lost to us, to the Change, while the children grow to adulthood and I wither, rejecting Change that calls stronger, ever stronger, until my skin can no longer contain me.

Dizziness sweeps over me. Louis grabs for my arm, misses and I fall, but slowly, as though some strange remote control has slowed us all—stretching out this moment and deadening sound. I can see their rounded mouths, widened eyes, three pairs of arms reaching, three pairs of legs striding. One tiny girl still at last, her head at a curious angle as though she's listening for something.

Sky and ground cartwheel crazily, then steady. I am out of their midst, away from the small crowd they make around a form on the ground. Sounds come crashing back, of wind thrashing in the trees, the whisper of tires as cars pass in the distant streets, meaningless noise.

I am light, light as the breath of a newborn babe, light as a dream. Even Change changes as the body wears out and the eyes dim. Not unpleasant, not to be avoided. My children cluster about the discarded, crumpled body I've finally shed, their mouths stiff and ugly in their shock, their lack of understanding. Too late now for all the things that might have been said, felt, shared over the years. Curiously, though, my lightness leaves little room for regret and none for sorrow at missed opportunities.

Green eyes, pale hair float tantalizingly just beyond the trees and I feel myself tugged in that direction. Robert has waited for me, is waiting now. I hesitate only a moment, thinking my farewells to the children, knowing their own Change waits with infinite patience.

I soar, dipping and twisting on the Halloween wind, away from the gathering darkness.

A Wilder Truth

Mari Hersh-Tudor

A sharp, wicked moon sliced the night sky. Hungry trees thrust their nearly denuded limbs upwards, as if pleading with that pale radiance to free their feet from the clay below. Thorns, twigs and other small creatures of forest detritus clung to the skirts of the trees, hampering them, dragging them down, anchoring them forever to the confining earth.

No breeze stirred that army of giants. No sound of hunt nor howl broke upon that air. No nightbird called; no cricket dared that angry silence. Everyone hid. Yet sound there was, enough and more to make up for the normal traffic thereabouts. One creature only caused the rest to go to ground, and *she* wasn't in the mood to notice.

She crashed heedlessly through the forest ahead of the hunters, underbrush catching and scratching at her, anger and humiliation blinding her to the roots that tripped her up, her family's rejection still ringing in her ears. *Different*, they'd spat at her, and *You're not one of us, go live with them.* As if she ever could. Leave them to join Them? Desert her family, just like that? Go to that cold foreign wilderness and live among savages? *It isn't fair!* she'd cried back at them, *I didn't ask for this, it just happened!* Father then said the last thing she wanted to hear from any of her beloved family. *There is no place in the family for one such as you.*

They turned on her and cast her out.

Breath whistling through her throat, she dropped down at the base of a tree to rest awhile, her ears straining through the panicked hiss of her breathing toward the sounds of pursuit. Nothing, so far. She lay panting, wishing she'd been born with the size and physical stamina her brothers and sisters enjoyed. Runt, the least of them, she'd learned very early to stay out of the way and amuse herself.

Maybe it was the singing that had made her different. Out of boredom, she'd sung more and better than they ever did, songs of glory and awe to the moon and stars, which had finally driven Father to come down hard on her, reminding her that there were ravening beasts out there who would kill them all when they found them by following her singing. She hadn't stopped singing; she was just very circumspect about it afterwards. Now her own desperate gasping echoed around her in tortured arrhythmia, jarring, any other aural evidence of life completely absent. Good. Maybe she'd outrun them after all.

A wild howl of triumph split the air—close, much closer than she expected. She bolted. How had they gotten so close? She hadn't heard a thing. She couldn't hear them now. All she could hear were the snap and rustle of her own panicked flight. *I should have known better,* she thought despairingly. *Father at least would never give up.*

There had been no mistaking the death sentence in their eyes when they'd driven her out, they who had once been all the love and trust that existed in her limited world. They had grown up together, strong and secure as a family should be. But she hadn't stopped growing. She'd grown right past them, right into the Change that had marked her as Other, threatening the family's unity, a blight on their honor.

That unity and honor were all that made her family function, all that stood between them and total anarchic disaster. They'd really had no choice but to rid themselves of her. Her family was like a trapped fox, she the leg caught in the steel jaws, holding them captive between worlds. So they'd cut her off, like the fox gnawing off his own leg when he hears the hunter's tread.

Where were her brothers and sisters? Surely they hadn't given up the chase so soon. Think, *think!* She mustn't let them sight her, or it would all be over except for the pain. She couldn't outrun them; she certainly couldn't outfight even one of them, much less all of them together. What could she do that they couldn't? What did she have that they lacked?

Change, that was what. Wits, too. She might not be as strong or as graceful as the rest of her family, but she'd figured out long ago that they lacked her capacity for long-range planning. Slowing her headlong run, she began casting about for a likely diversion, trying to ignore the persistent angry cries along her trail. *There! Water!* Father had lost a trail more than once in the deep, rushing stream.

She dove in, smothering a yelp as the frigid swell closed over her head.

Far downstream, her head broke the surface and she rode with the flow, catching a bit of breath back after her mindless flight through the forest, using the time as she tread water to think of further strategies. They'd expect her to go to the water. Weakened targets on the edge of panic would do so. How far downstream should she go? She was already out of the area her family habituated.

Having put some distance between herself and her pursuers, she now had to lose them. It would be no easy task; they were seasoned trackers. Resolve glittered in her eyes. Neither her family nor the legendary beasts would find her unless she chose.

Making a quick decision, she climbed out onto the far bank, dripping and shivering in the sudden chill. They would track her at least this far, but they would waste a lot of time combing the riverbanks for her trail. She had a good enough head start on them to lay some seriously confusing backtracks. Ducking and weaving through the trees, she used every bit of the woodlore they'd drilled into her to throw them off her tracks, dipping in and out of the stream again for good measure. Finally, she entered the water again, swimming strongly downstream and initiating the Change as she went.

Not much further along, she saw what she wanted: a tree hanging over the water. Grabbing hold, she climbed up. This was a gamble. Hopefully, none of her family would even fit on this little tree. Hopefully, they wouldn't even think to check it. Hopefully, even if they did, they wouldn't connect the new tracks with her. The last thing she wanted was for them to be able to track her in both of her forms. She lay very, very quietly along the trunk, listening very, very carefully.

There. Faint, and far behind her now—frustrated yells. It was working. She sighed, supposing that there was a lot that was far behind her now. But she wasn't going to take any chances. She glanced around curiously. The forest was denser here. All to the good. She took to the trees, moving from one to the other without ever touching the ground between. A growing sense of confidence in her escape made her reckless, and she misjudged a jump, crashing to the ground in a shower of dislodged leaves and twigs, changing back in sheer reflexive fright as she hit. She froze, huddling into herself for a terrified eternity in abject fear, hoping against hope that her careless move hadn't cost her her freedom and her life.

It seemed all of creation waited with her. Time slowed, and silence fled out like ripples in a pond around her, the pebble dropped in the center. Waves of quietude stilled the rustle of leaves and the creaking of limbs, calmed the voices of disturbed night creatures, halted the whisper and scrabble of a thousand small dramas played hourly in the microcosm of loam.

As the pounding of her heart—but not the ache of it—eased, she rose and made her way cautiously in the unfamiliar woods. She'd done plenty of exploring in both forms, but the new form was so strange, its perceptions so foreign, that well-known haunts became harsh and otherworldly. This place was completely new, she was pretty sure.

Lifting her head to the stars to orient herself, she saw the bright sickle moon shining friendly beams down on her and the songs welled up again in her throat, only to die in a whimper as she recalled that it wasn't just the "ravening beasts" who could find her that way. Of their own will, her feet turned towards her cache-place, a safe, dry area to hide human accoutrements while they weren't needed. So well-prepared. She hadn't been, the first time.

It had come on with her maturity. She'd run crying to her mother, asking, *Why does it hurt so?* Mother looked at her with the wary eyes of distrust, followed her when she ran and saw what happened to her when the moon was full. The whole family had come to her then, aghast at the beast their least daughter had become, and said, *Control yourself, or else.* Well, she'd tried to control herself, oh, how she tried, and in the process, learned that she could change whenever she wanted to, really. The more often she did so, the less overpowering the urge during the full moon.

She did it, quickly, changed and changed again right there on the path, just to prove she could. In fact, if she could have known, she was one of the most talented of her kind that way.

Her skin shivered with delayed shock at the Change. There was a decided difference in the comfort factor between fur and skin. Fur, even damp fur, was better for traveling in the woods on a cold, crisp night. Padding silently along the well-remembered trail to her cache-place under a crumbling overpass, she made and discarded a dozen plans for her future.

Now that she moved with purpose, the forest itself gave way before her. The green-black canopy overhead bent aside for moonlit lances tracing a path ever further from the forest's heart. Small sounds accompanied her passage. Excited whisperings flanked the path; a thousand breathless chitterings strove behind, before, beyond. Timbered groves leaned to watch in their ageless, ponderous fashion. Caught in the cusp of Change, turning on the pivot of transformation, they knew only that a Power passed them by.

In a way, she'd been preparing for the inevitable confrontation for some time, playing at surviving in the woods as a human (not very easy), and in the city as a wolf (much easier). Most humans were pretty stupid about large canines. She usually got labeled a Malamute or a Husky, with a few perceptive ones declaring she must be a wolf-dog hybrid. Sometimes she had a hard time not showing them just what kind of a hybrid she was.

Some of the homeless knew her secret, but she wasn't worried. She'd practiced among them, learned from them, honed her skills protecting those she cared about from casual criminals, who abounded in the forgotten parts of the city. Oh, yes, she had basic survival skills in both forms, she'd made sure of that.

A wolf ghosting through the outskirts of the city looked to the casual eye like anybody's pet out for a stroll. Tame vegetation surrounded her now, pale shadows of former glory beaten into submission by a population unwilling to confront the wilder truth outside their bland, ordered world. Timid trees grew as and where they were bid in woody apology for intruding their life and breath on this massive, unnatural jungle. The further she went into the city, the more these trees became cowed and frightened, the more this grass cringed beneath her feet, the more the very air cried foul. She was getting close now.

It wasn't until she was there at the cache-place, had been there for some time staring at her clothing spread around her, hesitating halfway between forms, that she made her decision at last.

A new form for a new life. She had been given those strange, gangling limbs as a gift, learned to use them, couldn't stop using them when so ordered, now she must gather them up and embrace this cruel, alien world.

Head high, fully clothed, she rose up on two legs and strode into the city.

Breaking the Circle

Michael W. Lucas

"I told you a five-eighths! This is a five-sixteenths!"

Father wouldn't have been mad, if she'd just done it right. Chris rummaged through the big toolbox. The greasy wrenches and screwdrivers were all churned together, and escaped her touch. She finally caught a larger wrench and handed it to Father.

Chris and her father were taking off the old basement door. She had almost clawed through it last time. The new door stood at an angle against the kitchen sink. Chris was sixteen years old. Hair was starting to grow on her face.

Of the many times Chris had been locked in the basement, she remembered the first time the best. Her twelfth birthday had hit only days before, and Father had actually laughed and sung and got her a junkyard bicycle he'd repaired and repainted. He'd hugged her, too. Mom had patted Chris on the head and told her "Happy Birthday."

That had been the last time anyone had touched her. It was also the last time that Father had been kind to her.

Chris was sweeping the bathroom's dusty tile after dinner when she noticed the hair on her hands. It was white and soft, like the first shoots of spring grass. Her hands had always been hairless; they'd been smooth an hour before. Her stomach squirmed around the peanut butter sandwich she'd had for dinner. She suddenly itched, everywhere.

The cracked bathroom mirror diagonally split her reflection. Short albino hair had appeared across her forehead and under her chin. She quivered, and hair sprouted below her eyes and spread across her cheeks.

Mom had come in then, probably to tell Chris to turn off the light and stop staring in the mirror. Mom's face was even thinner than Chris's, and just as pale. Her eyes grew wide when she saw Chris caressing her furry face, then she turned and dashed through the hall towards the living room.

Chris turned back to the mirror. Her face felt unfamiliar, as if it belonged to someone else.

Father shouted from the living room, "She's what?" Chris cringed. Father was drunk, of course. He'd been drunk for months, gulping his government benefits for not working the farm. He wasn't used to not working. It was hard on him. "This wouldn't have happened if you'd had a boy!"

Mom murmured something, too soft for Chris to hear. Father screamed, "She got it from *your* grandmother! You take care of your freak child! I never would've married you if I'd thought this was going to happen!"

Chris turned away from the mirror and pulled the string for the light. She should be scrubbing the floor when Mom saw her again, or trying to wash the walls without tearing off yet another strip of cheap wallpaper. Mom had wanted new wallpaper for as long as Chris remembered, paper that didn't peel off the walls.

She snatched the bucket from under the sink and dropped it into the claw-foot iron bathtub. She would wash the floor; then Mom would see that she hadn't meant to be staring in the mirror, she'd only stopped on the way to get the bucket, she was responsible, really. She would ignore the fierce itching, the sudden urge to nibble on her lower lip.

She had just turned the clammy faucet for cold water when Mom reappeared in the doorway. "Chris, honey."

Chris turned to face her. *Don't frown, and don't smile.* If she smiled, Mom would think she was laughing at her.

"Why don't you go down to the basement and play for awhile?"

The basement only had one light bulb, dangling from the naked rafters, and smelled even more mildewy than the rest of the house. Spiders ruled most of it. Father sent her downstairs when she'd been bad.

Chris wanted to cry. "Okay."

Mom stepped back, watching Chris in the same way that she often looked at Dad. Chris didn't like it. She hadn't done anything. Why was Mom staring like that?

Chris walked past her mother, conscious of those eyes on her back. They went through the dusty family room, avoiding the doorway to the back room where Father sat in his big chair. She heard an aluminum can clatter; Father had thrown an empty beer can at the television.

"Dad's upset, just ignore him. I'll make you a couple sandwiches," Mom said quickly, softly. "Would you like some ham?"

Chris blinked. The ham was Father's. "I...is it okay?"

"Of course it's okay! I said you could, didn't I?"

"Thank you, Mom."

Chris's ragged sneakers always stuck to the kitchen tile, no matter how often she washed it. The table's bad leg was slightly askew again. She'd have to straighten it before it fell over and Mom and Dad yelled at her. She stood quietly by the basement door while Mom opened the fridge and took out a plastic bag of deli ham and a loaf of bread. When Mom quickly slapped three sandwiches together, with more ham and cheese than Dad ever got, Chris's eyes grew wide. And a pickle, too?

Mom wrapped everything in paper towels and shoved them in Chris's hands. "You go downstairs now, all right, honey?" Mom's smile was tight, and she kept glancing over her shoulder towards the back room.

Chris nodded. "All right, Mom."

Mom's smile relaxed a little, and she reached out as if to pat Chris's head. She jerked her hand back, however, and that careful look returned to her eyes. "Just you do as I say, and everything'll be okay." Mom said that at least once a day.

Chris walked down the stairs. The old wood creaked under her weight. When she was at the bottom and had pulled the string for the light, Mom pushed the door closed. Chris flinched when she heard the heavy deadbolt click into place.

"Hold it! Hold it, I said!" Father inhaled another mouthful of whiskey, picked up the black marker and turned to the gaping doorway.

Chris struggled to hold the four-inch square beam level as Father traced the ends on either side of the doorframe. He wanted to mount a heavy hinge on one side and a bracket on the other. Father said that when they finished, a bull could hit that door without making it quiver.

They had about four hours to get the new door installed. Maybe less.

The cracks in the irregular cinder-block walls made Chris shiver.

They always looked like they were going to crash inwards in a flood of dirt and worms and something else, she didn't know what, but something filthy and with many teeth.

Chris's whole body had begun to itch, and she set the sandwiches down on the washtub to try to scratch her back. She couldn't reach the itch. Finally she picked up a twisted ruler from the concrete floor, checked it for anything crawling, and used it to claw between her shoulder blades.

But her legs itched too, and her arms and her face, and even her tiny breasts. She scratched and scratched and abruptly found herself on the ground, scratching everywhere, twisting to touch all of herself at once. Her jaw began to hurt; she must have banged herself on the floor and not noticed. Her teeth ached, too.

The itching stopped suddenly, as if someone had thrown a switch. Chris sat up to catch her breath. Dad was shouting again. She could hear his voice through the floor, even though she didn't understand his words.

Mom cares about me, Chris thought. *That's why she sent me downstairs and locked me in. Mom thought I'd be happier down here.*

Dad cares, too. I know he does.

Lining one wall were rusty metal shelves covered with old bottles and books and parts of appliances that Father kept saying he'd fix. His big toolbox was a blocky shape beside the shelves. A narrow window faced east, just above ground level. From there, Chris could see the chicken coop, empty since a fox had taken them all. The sky was already turning dark blue with the coming night.

Night? Chris shivered. Mom didn't want her to stay down here all night, did she? She suddenly noticed the complex smells of mildew and rust blending together. They seemed stronger than they ever had before. There was no place to sit down, no place to get away from the spiders. She didn't see any spiders right now, but they would come out as soon as she relaxed.

The itching returned, even more strongly than before. Chris felt hair creeping out of her skin. She immediately forgot the spiders and fell down to scratch herself on the concrete floor. The bloated moon was low enough to fill the window, and seemed to be smiling at her.

Her jaw hurt even more. Her teeth abruptly felt sharp, then her shirt seemed to shrink and choke her, her pants twisted away from her skin, and the itch, the itch everywhere. She tore at her shirt, popping buttons, and finally ripped it off and flung it. The fur on her hands was gray now, and thicker, but she hardly noticed as she attacked her belt. The plastic threatened to cut her in half, and she scrabbled at the buckle with stubby fingers until it opened and she squeezed out of her pants.

Chris's hips had changed too, and they *hurt!* She rolled onto all fours, trying to get up, struggling to walk, quivering. She felt hot; she should have been sweating, but she wasn't.

Father wanted her to hold the crossbeam steady so he could drill guide holes for the screws. She understood, but the big piece of wood weighed more than she did and it shook horribly with the drill. Father didn't help; he was too intent on drilling as deep as he could, using hard shoves on the drill. Chris smelled smoking insulation. Father didn't notice.

Yesterday, one of the boys at school had asked her to go to the spring dance with him. Her belly had burned at the thought, and she wanted to stammer "yes." Her skin had itched from underneath, though, and the night before, the moon had hung gibbous, so she'd said that she wouldn't be free tonight and turned away.

Chris held the wood as firmly as she could. Thankfully, it was steady enough.

The basement suddenly had become less scary. The simple smells were a tapestry of sensation, telling her more than she ever thought possible. The concrete hurt her paws. Circling, she moved like a race car, always hoping to find a way out of the hole, and never finding it.

The smell drifting through the windows, marking the fields and woods, maddened her and made her claw at the brick beneath the window. She wanted to leap up and squeeze through the tiny portal, but it was too high and too narrow.

When she tried clawing and scratching at the door, bits of the old wood broke away under her claws. She threw herself against the door repeatedly, but it only rattled in the doorframe.

The meat in the sandwiches tantalized her, but the smell of the processing made her turn away. She couldn't eat the pickle either, even though something in her remembered liking them.

She heard voices upstairs. Each word was distinct, but none

meant anything. She barked for their attention. The voices stopped, then began again.

When Mom opened the door the next morning, Chris was naked, sleeping curled up on her clothes. For once, she didn't have to do her chores that day.

The new door was up. Four inches thick. Solid oak. The old dead-bolt was uselessly warped, and the doorframe was cracked. Father had set the new hinge and latch in support beams to either side of the doorframe. The crossbeam stood upright on its hinge, ready to drop into the latch and bar the door. Chris had seen similar doors on TV, late at night. They kept all sorts of monsters out.

By the second month, a routine had been established. Hair grew on Chris's face and neck. Mom made her something to eat, and asked her to go downstairs. The deadbolt clicked.

Mom became thinner. Father became louder. Chris knew that he cared—he wouldn't yell if he didn't care—but she wished that he'd be nice, just once in a while.

In September, she had gone to school the day before the night. The other students laughed at the soft hair on her face and hands, and she was sent home early. Mom didn't ask why but stopped making her go to school when she didn't get out of bed.

On the days she stayed home from school, Father drank even more. He either mumbled at the floor or shouted for Chris to bring him another beer. His eyes were bloodshot and hard when she brought the sweating cans, and he stared coldly at her without saying anything.

It's my fault, Chris thought. *Something's wrong with me.*

Sometimes Chris dreamed of telling her father to be quiet, telling her mother that she wanted to go out under the moon. Father would have yelled at her, though, and Mom would have shaken her head and said, "You shouldn't," with a hint of tears. They knew what they were doing.

In the tenth grade, on her first day of woodworking class, Chris found herself staring at a razor knife in her hand. The fluorescent light glinted blue and white on the cutting edge, parallel to her bony fingers. It's wrong, she thought. It should rip, tear, not slice.

She shuddered. That afternoon, Chris quit the woodworking class and signed up for Modern English. At the end of the semester, she brought her report card home, covered with *A*'s and a *B*. Father looked at the report card and said, "I thought you were taking woodworking? You signed up for woodworking, didn't you? Go to your room!"

Mom smiled thinly, and said that she'd done well. "Just ignore your father, he's had a bad day."

More and more often, Mom gave her those Father-looks. Chris began spending long hours walking through the fields and woods, looking at the wildlife and wondering what it would all smell like.

Circling in the basement, she had somehow remembered the sensation of opened arteries spilling into her mouth, the toughness of gristle in her teeth. She'd never had meat that fresh. Still, it seemed right. The moon shone through the window, and she wanted to run through the woods and play tag with it, find a good spot of ground to make her own and mark her fur with its scent.

She circled again and again, almost swallowing her own tail. Claws ticked on concrete. *The voices overhead hold me in this hole,* she thought. The scent of woods edged through the window. Splinters of door covered the stairs.

They *still* wouldn't let her out.

The door was getting thin.

Father grabbed the crossbeam and dropped it into the U-shaped latch, then tugged on the handle with all his weight. The door didn't even rattle. "That'll hold."

You, Chris silently finished.

Father clenched his whiskey bottle and shuffled towards the front of the house. "Pick up the tools and put them downstairs."

The wrenches, hammers and screwdrivers were scattered over half the kitchen, greasing the ancient tile. She'd have to wash the floor.

This door looked much more solid than the old one. Chris remembered gouging the door until her claws and teeth bled, until the door had been thin enough to punch a single claw through. She felt ill with disappointment. It was going to be worse tonight.

Chris threw a pair of wrenches into the toolbox. Father had gone through all of the screwdrivers before finding one that fit the screws on the bracket. She put the screwdrivers away one at a time, until she held the last one in her hand: the one Father had used to turn the four heavy screws into the beam. Father had tightened them so forcefully that the bracket had sunk into the wood.

Circling.

It wasn't right, holding something trapped.

Scratching.

With a trembling hand, Chris fumbled the screwdriver up to the bracket. One screw would hold it in place long enough to fool Father. Just one night, one night under the moon.

Biting.

Chris stopped, dimly remembering the taste of meat, the tear of a gristly throat. She couldn't...wouldn't....

Tears came to her eyes, and she blinked them away. She rubbed one side of her face with a grimy hand, then dropped the screwdriver into the toolbox. She crouched and grabbed the handle. The toolbox shifted, and she felt her back muscles tighten. She pulled harder, and one side of the box rose an inch.

She stood, looking at the stairs, then back towards the living room. "Father?"

"What?" he shouted.

"I've got a problem."

She heard a muffled curse, then his footsteps tromped closer. "What?" he asked as he came through the door.

"I picked up the tools, but I can't lift them."

"Goddamn girl," he growled, then snatched up the box with one hand. "You get something and clean up the floor."

She watched Father sidle down the stairs, moving heavily with the tools. Before she knew it, her hand had swung out and slammed the door. The other hand swung the crossbeam into place.

She still had time to wash the floor before the moon rose.

Wilding

Melanie Tem

Pam was in Lydia's house again. This time, Lydia had invited her in. The profound risk, the nearly incredible defiance, frightened her. The fear excited her and made her angry—with her mother and daughter and grandmother, with Pam.

"Want a ride home?" Pam had asked her as they'd left the store together well after closing.

Lydia had tried to decipher bus schedules when she'd left her car at the shop that morning, had finally concluded that she'd have to walk downtown and catch a bus home from there rather than trying to transfer. Defeated, she'd thought irritably of Deborah, who apparently took buses all the time, and of her mother, who used to be able to go anywhere in the city on foot but who now could get lost within a block of their houses. "No, thanks," she'd told Pam. "I can walk."

Pam had put an arm around her, so·briefly that Lydia hadn't had time to react. But her head had been buzzing with the sweetness and danger of the embrace, and she'd had trouble focusing when Pam had said cheerfully, "Don't be silly. Walk home with me and we'll get Friedrich and the car. Friedrich loves to ride in the car."

Friedrich had been beside himself with pleasure to see Pam, and had yelped happily at Lydia, too. Pam had crouched, taken his long-eared head in both hands, and nuzzled him. Lydia had actually found herself bending to pet him, too, very tentatively and quickly. On the ride to her house, he'd braced his hind legs on the edge of the back seat and his front legs on the headrest behind Lydia, stretching his long little body, his breath warm and faintly rancid. "Friedrich *loves* going for a ride," Pam had observed again, smiling. "Do you have pets, Lydia?"

Lydia had laughed before she could stop herself, then said, "No."

Suddenly worried, Pam had glanced at her. "I never thought to ask if you minded him coming with us. He's so much a part of my life that I forget other people may not think he's as wonderful as I do. Sorry."

Friedrich had snuffled against the back of her neck and licked her once. She'd winced and shuddered, but said, "It's okay."

Stopped for the light at Forty-fourth, Pam had reached across to pet Friedrich and brushed Lydia's hair. Lydia had thought Pam's fingers rested there a split second longer than necessary, but they'd been gone before she could fully register the lingering or what it could possibly mean. The dog had made curious little moans of ecstasy as Pam stroked him. Then the light had changed and Pam had put both hands back on the wheel to turn south onto Federal. Lydia had kept herself very still, thinking against her will how starved she was for human contact, how the need had not at all diminished with time and neglect, and how utterly vulnerable that made her.

"Nothing from Deborah?"

"She called."

Pam drew her breath in sharply. "Oh, thank God. What did she say?"

"She said she hates me, all of us. She said she's never coming home."

"I'm sorry, Lydia," Pam said, and then, mercifully, said no more about Deborah. Already it seemed to Lydia that her daughter had moved into her past, and that she would surely never see her again. After a slight pause, Pam asked, "Which house do you want to go to?"

The fact that Pam would think to ask the question had startled Lydia a little. It seemed arcane, intimate knowledge that there were four family houses around a central walled courtyard, and that she might be expected to go to any of them. Although she'd probably herself told Pam enough for all of this to be apparent, Lydia had wondered uneasily, hopefully, what else the other woman already knew about her.

"Mine," she'd said. "On Harvey." And then, when Pam had pulled the car over to the curb—as Lydia had seen, to her obsessive chagrin, the dry and untrimmed grass along the front walk, the gutter pulling loose from the eaves—she'd found herself rushing headlong to ask, "Would you—do you have time to come in?"

So now she was standing on the first landing—dust on the uncarpeted edges of the stairs although she'd washed them just last week, a hair-line crack she hadn't noticed before in the wallpaper beside the door—and Pam and the nosy, distressingly charming little dog were actually in the entryway of her house, and she had absolutely no idea what to say or do next.

"This is a beautiful old house," Pam was saying, looking around.

Lydia wanted to cry out, *Don't do that! Don't look around!* But that would be silly. But since she loathed the house, it would also be silly to say thank you.

"It must be a lot to take care of," Pam said. "I have enough trouble keeping up with my apartment, and there's just Friedrich and me. Do you do it all yourself?"

"All four of them," Lydia admitted.

Pam stared. "All four houses? By yourself?"

"I don't do a very good job," Lydia said.

"You do a *great* job!" Pam protested. "You take care of *everybody!* But, Lydia, who takes care of you?"

Lydia was speechless. Pam had moved to the foot of the stairs and Lydia was now on the first step, so the two women had come quite close to each other. Pam's bright brown eyes and generous mouth were at the level of Lydia's breasts, almost touching them.

"I admire you," Pam told her softly. "And I worry about you."

Lydia took the step down to the floor. Friedrich had settled himself in front of the last riser, and when she stepped over him his fur was silky against the back of her ankle. Easily, Pam put her arms around her. Holding her breath, Lydia allowed her cheek to rest very lightly on the top of the curly head.

"If there's anything I can do, I'm here," Pam murmured, stroking Lydia's back. The rhythmic motion both hurt and soothed. "I am your friend, you know."

Then Lydia felt Pam's small, sturdy body pull away. Certain she'd done something foolish, she started to pull away herself, stiff and trembling with the embarrassment of anticipated rejection.

But Pam reached up, took her face in both hands, and kissed her full on the mouth. Sweetly, lingeringly. Lips parted just a little, breath warm.

Lydia couldn't breathe. Her heart beat wildly against Pam's, which she could feel beating hard, too, but steadily, regularly. Lydia's throat constricted as if she would cry, which, of course, she would not. "I—

I have to—go check—" she stammered, and pushed around Pam toward the kitchen.

"I'll come with you. I might be able to help with her."

"No!" Pam looked at her, startled. Lydia managed to control herself enough to say relatively calmly, "No, she's very old and sick and she doesn't want anybody outside the family in her house."

"Will you be long?" Pam smiled. "Shall I wait?"

Recklessly, Lydia answered, "Yes, please wait," and fled through the house, out the door, and across the courtyard to her grandmother's dark house.

Her grandmother wasn't there.

Wasn't anywhere.

Lydia searched the mother house first, called, sniffed, looked and listened in every room and every denlike cranny of the complicated old structure. Then she searched the houses on the north and south sides of the courtyard, facing Thirty-second and Thirty-third Avenues, the houses where no one had lived, really, since her great-aunts had been murdered there; in the basements their cracked skulls leered downward, sideways, utterly uninterested in her.

Standing in one place and shading her eyes, she searched the courtyard. Panic-stricken now, hardly thinking at all, searching instinctively but with tangled and unreliable instincts. Aware there was terrible danger but unsure of its exact source or nature: Pam discovering Mary, Mary killing Pam, both or either of them leaving her.

In her house, she looked through the unused back room, then in the kitchen where the sink was full of dirty dishes even though she'd done a load that morning, then ran up the narrow winding back stairs where the dust lay thick as fur, onto the second floor, through her bedroom, Deborah's bedroom, hardly thinking *Deborah* but afraid for her daughter, too, (who wasn't anywhere, either), the bathroom with the clawfoot tub, the unused room at the end of the hall, up the stairs to the attic, through the nearly bare attic to the room her grandmother used under the eaves at the far east end. Mary was nowhere to be found.

Realizing with a plummeting stomach that she hadn't looked in the basement, Mary could at this moment be slinking up the basement steps toward Pam or hiding down there waiting to see what would happen next, Lydia raced down the three flights, nearly falling, nearly losing her breath altogether, and searched through all the half rooms and open areas of the basement. Years and years of accumulated dirt and dung, some of it fresh. Boxes of clothes, boxes of plastic dishes, bags of newspapers, cans for some reason without labels. The odors and noises of other creatures, but not Mary.

Mary was not here. Mary was gone.

They would say it was her fault. It was her fault.

"Lydia?"

Pam was coming down the basement stairs. Lydia could hardly believe it. Friedrich stood behind her in the doorway to the kitchen, peering down and whimpering, unwilling to try the steep, dark incline. Pam, though, was already halfway down, setting her feet carefully on the rickety steps and holding on to both the railing and the wall, but looking at her.

"Lydia? Are you all right? What's wrong?"

"Wait! Wait, I'm coming up."

In the seconds it took for her to get to Pam, Lydia realized all in a flash: Her grandmother was gone. Her daughter was gone. Her mother and Marguerite and all the cousins from the mountains were gone. For the moment or for the rest of their lives, she and Pam were alone.

"Wait," she said again, this time meaning *don't leave* although Pam showed no signs of leaving other than having retreated back up into the kitchen. "Nothing—nothing's wrong. My grandmother is—sleeping. Would you—would you like to stay for dinner?"

She made a spinach quiche. It surprised her that she remembered how; no one in her family would eat anything so exotic, but Jake used to like it and she did still remember. Pam liked her cooking. Pam still sat across the kitchen table from her when the quiche and the tossed salad were gone and they were sipping the white wine Lydia had remembered in the top cupboard. Friedrich snored between their feet. Pam sighed contentedly and said, "That was wonderful. Thank you. You're a really good cook. Your family is lucky to have you."

Pleased out of all proportion, distrusting her own pleasure, Lydia did say, "Thank you."

The single glass of wine, the imminent and profound danger, the ease of Pam's company were all so heady and arousing that after a time Lydia wondered if maybe *this* was how she would, after all, transform. Not into a were-creature but out of one, for all her life she'd been a sort of were-woman, no more fully human than fully anything else. Maybe she would transform into her true nature by falling in love. With a woman. With this woman, with Pam Sandahl. She had not thought it possible.

The house was very quiet. All four houses and their courtyard were quiet. No one else was there. Lydia brewed coffee, not nearly as strong as her mother and grandmother took it in the morning, and she and Pam carried cups of it and plates of brownies into the living room. Lydia considered the living room tacky and was embarrassed to have her friend there: The elegant beige drapes were threadbare at the scalloped edges, the carved wooden mantlepiece badly needed refinishing. But Pam exclaimed, "What a charming room!" and—hesitantly, not sure what she was agreeing to—Lydia agreed.

Lydia sat on the long brocade couch. Pam came and sat beside her. Trotting along behind, Friedrich looked longingly at the matching chair in the corner by the bookcase but couldn't jump high enough, so he contented himself with stretching out on the carpet, dark brown on lighter brown. Lydia saw, to her dismay, wolf fur adhered in the whorls of the carpet, even though she vacuumed every carpet in all four houses every day.

They finished coffee and dessert without saying much. Lydia kept an ear cocked for footsteps, breathing, but she heard nothing, and among all the odors of the house she didn't smell her mother or her grandmother. She was sure no one else was here. She couldn't understand it. She couldn't understand her own reaction, either, and she knew how dangerous it was; while she was nervous, tingling with tension, her head was also light with the sensation of freedom.

They were holding hands.

Pam's head was resting against her shoulder.

Pam's hand was gently turning her face, and they were kissing.

After a long, slow moment, Lydia tentatively brought her hand to the back of Pam's head and tangled her fingers in the soft curls, careful not to hurt her with her nails. Late afternoon, late summer sunlight came in still high through the western windows and spread across them—today's sunlight, the sunlight of a hundred years ago.

Pam's hands were on the small of Lydia's back, inside her shirt on her hardening nipples, between her legs. Without taking her mouth off Pam's, without closing her eyes, Lydia unbuttoned the other woman's silky blouse and slid it off. Pam's breasts, shoulders, belly were round and smooth.

Lydia and her lover held each other, caressed each other, arms and legs wrapped around each other and cream-colored, golden, rosy, dark brown in the marbled sunshine, mouths to each other's bodies, voices and breathing raised. The house pulsed with the pungent scent of female sex. Lydia wanted, *wanted,* and Pam was murmuring Lydia's name. Pam slid her open mouth down Lydia's body— breasts, navel, labia. Resisting the impulse to hold her breath, Lydia breathed deeply and rhythmically, and with each inhalation and exhalation her arousal deepened.

Then, not wanting to, she half heard, half smelled someone else in the house. Lydia looked and saw them, but Pam did not. Lydia cried out, and her lover gave a muted answering cry of passion, or love.

From the hallway, Ruth roared and leapt.

The lovers separated, screamed, reached for each other. Lydia cried, "Ma!"

A small brown form threw itself against Ruth's chest, yipping frenziedly, thinly growling. It was enough to distract Ruth's attention and deflect the attack. Pam shrieked, "Friedrich!"

Ruth swiped at the dog, lifted him skewered on her claws, and sank her teeth into his throat. He howled. She howled. She flung him down and broke open his rib cage with one easy blow, removed his heart and ate it. Then she pushed aside the bleeding carcass and dropped to all fours. Another beast was beside her, huge and hump-shouldered, growling. Marguerite. Together they advanced.

"Ma!" Lydia heard herself cry again. "Oh, Ma!"

Pam gasped, "Lydia!"

Ruth's feral gaze was fixed and yellow. Lydia had seen that look infrequently from her mother, but had feared and coveted it all her life. Nearly a wolf, with nearly human eyes.

Lydia was half-clothed. Her breasts swelled with the fresh memory of Pam's hands and mouth on them. Her nipples were bright pink nubs, hurting from interrupted and redirected passion. The engorged areolae, ringed with dark bristling hairs, were tingling. Her heart pounded savagely, making her dizzy, thrilling her with its power, opening and closing its valves, pumping her blood through its four chambers and sending it, changed, coursing back out through her body again, through her brain.

Pam's frilly white blouse was open over her large breasts and round belly, its tails framing her buttocks in back and the golden-brown mound of curly pubic hair in front. The soft trail of hair was vivid, leading up the smooth expanse of her abdomen to her navel, where Lydia's moistened fingertips had probed just moments before.

Pam's face shone with tears. Friedrich lay just beyond her reach at the feet of the wolf, still quivering. His blood shone like her tears, as did the fluids that bathed his exposed and ruptured intestines, as did the semiliquid excrement that spread over the fine wooden floor and the opened cavity where his heart had been.

Lydia's nostrils flared and saliva gathered in her mouth, well beyond her control. "No!" she cried, and then whispered, *"Yes."*

Marguerite shouldered past her cousin. Her single eye glittered yellow. The other socket was an equally vivid black. Lydia's mother turned her head, obviously losing her concentration, growled, "No."

As had happened once before in her life—when she'd come home with Deborah *(Deborah)*—the realization came abrupt and fully formed into her mind: *This is her chance.* But this time she understood, with a painful rush of adrenaline, that the chance was her own.

The chance to choose.

The chance to inhabit fully one nature or another.

The chance to save someone she loved and set her free, or to devour her.

Either way, to be, at last, transformed.

Lydia shivered with indecision.

Pam moved against her. Pressed against her, her back against Lydia's chest. Not looking at Pam's back now or touching it, Lydia so vividly remembered the feel of it that her tongue itched from the inside out and her breath came ragged out of her throat. Terror, rage, and intense sexual arousal raced along the pathways of her nervous system between her skin and her flesh, burning new pathways, exploding into new synapses carrying new messages. Lydia trembled.

She felt hair forcing itself out through her pores, saw it darken her thighs, her arms, her breasts until it hung down itching over her abdomen. She tasted her own blood as her teeth elongated and punctured her gums and bottom lip. She heard the sudden alteration of sounds—how clear they became, how they multiplied, how she knew what each was without naming it. She smelled the sudden wild proliferation of odors. Her eyes ached from their abrupt perception of colors she had never seen before.

More herself than she'd ever been, Lydia found herself lowering her head, which was longer and heavier now, and putting her mouth to the back of Pam's neck, which was exposed to her under damp curls. Tendons buzzed, sprang back against her dry lips and tongue. Soft flesh rose into her teeth.

"Lydia, I love you!" Pam pleaded, and then managed to turn to face her. Her eyes widened at the sight of Lydia, so close. "My God, what *are* you?"

I love you.

Fur retracted back under the skin, hurting. Fangs pushed painfully back into their sockets, and again Lydia tasted blood. Physical sensation dulled while thoughts and emotions vivified. Once again, Lydia was more herself than she'd ever been, this time more fully human.

Again she bent over her lover. Pam tried to pull away and almost fell off the couch. She clutched at Lydia to keep from tumbling backward into the reach of the wolf.

Lydia caught her easily, steadied her. She pressed the aching pads of her palms against Pam's naked sides, intending to hold and protect her. But her nails raked the soft flesh and drew blood.

Pam cried out. Lydia cried out, said Pam's name. Said, "I love you."

Lydia lifted the smaller woman in her arms. Not recognizing this as protection, Pam shrieked and fought, managing to slam the back of Lydia's wrist hard against the edge of the fireplace. Pain and then numbness shot through Lydia's fingers, and her grip loosened enough that Pam got free and tried to run for the door.

Ruth snarled but didn't move, as if she didn't know what to do. Marguerite simply leaned into Pam's path and pushed her roughly back into Lydia's arms.

Mary didn't show herself. But Lydia heard her now, smelled her.

Deborah, of course, hadn't come home. But her presence, her absence, the impossible demands she made, were as palpable as the stench of all of them in this house, the stench of all the years and of Lydia herself, of Pam.

Marguerite said clearly, "Eat."

Pam reached up and touched Lydia's face. Her hurting, misshapen face, too round and soft for a wolf's and too angular for a woman's. "Love me," she said.

Thinking somehow she could obey them both and she wouldn't have to choose, Lydia bent and pressed her face into Pam's breasts. Pam's heart was kept from her now only by a thin layer of skin and flesh and delicate bone. She kissed the breast, the nipple, the heart. Her own heart swelled.

Her mother growled. "Lydia. Now."

Her lover called her name.

Lydia could not bear it. She couldn't choose, and her rage at being forced to choose, her terror, was unbearable. She would not choose. She would not participate. She would leave them all, and they could do whatever they were going to do without her.

Lydia let Pam fall between Ruth and Marguerite, on her back on the floor with throat, body, genitals exposed. She heard Pam's breath leave her body under the force of the impact and the massive presence of the two advancing wolves. She saw Marguerite's muzzle drop between Pam's spread legs.

Lydia howled. She leapt past the others, slipping and leaving her footprints in the blood that slicked the floor. She lunged against the door and wrested it open. Warm twilight air assaulted her, nearly blinded her. She ran out of the house, off the front porch, down the steps, out the gate, into the street.

Neither wolf nor woman, Lydia ran away. She did not choose. In the house she left behind, the heart of her lover was devoured by someone else.

About the Authors

Paul Allen, a blind author, lives and writes in the picturesque New England countryside with his wife and their two teenage children. Fallon, the inspiration for Lyka and a purebred black German shepard, is his third dog guide. He has been writing exclusively for the past five years and is a graduate of the 1994 Clarion West Science Fiction and Fantasy Writers Workshop. Fallon also attended Clarion West.

Judy Brewer shares her life in Riverton, Utah with her childhood sweetheart and best friend (to whom she's been married twenty-six years), four children, two grandchildren and a generous annual allotment of sixth graders. Two shelties, two gerbils, two cats, a canary and an iguana also occupy the residence. She loves Broadway musicals, reading, playing flute, painting, cheering for the Utah Jazz, and has been known, on occasion, to howl at the moon.

Renée M. Charles lives in a houseful of cats, has a B.A. in English and also teaches writing. She has had over one hundred stories, poems and articles published in over fifty genre magazines and anthologies, including *Weird Tales, Twilight Zone* and *2 AM.*

Suzy McKee Charnas lives and writes in New Mexico, where she moved with her husband in 1969. She writes science fiction, fantasy, and nonfiction articles and essays, occasionally teaches writing, and is best known for her futuristic, feminist epic begun with *Walk to the End of the World* and including the recently published third volume *The Furies,* and for her novel *The Vampire Tapestry,* the third chapter of which won a Nebula Award. Her latest work is a novella,

Beauty and the Opera, or the Phantom Beast, published in *Asimov's* and soon to be available in the anthology *Modern Classics of Fantasy* from Tor Books.

Steve Eller holds a degree in computer science and worked as a programmer analyst for many years before trying his hand at writing. In the first year and a half of his career, he's had forty stories accepted for publication in markets such as *Terminal Fright, Sinister, Wetware* and *A Horror Story a Day.* He reluctantly resides in Pennsylvania.

Barbara J. Ferrenz wrote humorous and off-beat short-shorts as a regular contributor to the now-defunct *Iguana Informer.* She has written two unpublished horror novels, and her agent is currently marketing *Worse Than Death,* the first in a mystery series featuring a writer of erotic vampire novels. Her short story, "Burb Vamp," will be appearing in the anthology *365 Scary Stories* (1997). She lives with her family in southern Maryland.

Mari Hersh-Tudor is a native of small-town lower Michigan and lives in the far northwest corner of Nebraska. When not writing, she is a model and artist looking forward to a dual-career painting covers for books she has written. When Mari grows up, she wants to be a drummer and work in Jim Henson's creature shop.

Charlee Jacob is a native Texan and lives in the Dallas-Fort Worth Metroplex with her husband Jim. She has had over one hundred stories and over two hundred poems accepted for publication in the last four years. She has work forthcoming in *Deathrealm, Terminal Fright* and *Bending the Landscape.* She has just finished a novel, *Dark Moods.*

Pamela J. Jessen has been writing on and off for several years. She has had stories published in *Twilight Zone, The Horror Show* and *Cemetery Dance,* and has a chapbook from Roadkill Press. Her writing has benefited from the sage, and sometimes not-so-sage, advice of her two critique groups and from Lois Hayna, poet and teacher.

Jeremy E. Johnson is the editor of *Stygian Articles*, a rewarding job that gives him the opportunity to work with fantastic authors, poets and artists, as well as three highly talented editors. He's earned a B.A. in English, with honors, and managed to get enough credits for a certificate in Film Studies. He's getting married in December to his love of seven years. His publishing credits include *Heliocentric Net, Aberrations* and *The Tome,* among others.

Ursula K. Le Guin was born in 1929 in Berkeley, California, where she grew up. Her parents were the anthropologist Alfred Kroeber and the writer Theodora Kroeber, author of *Ishi.* She went to Radcliffe College and did graduate work at Columbia University. She is married to Charles A. Le Guin, a historian. They live in Portland, Oregon, and have three children and two grandchildren. She has published over eighty short stories, two collections of essays, ten books for children, several volumes of poetry, and sixteen novels. Among the honors her writing has received are a National Book Award, five Hugo and four Nebula awards, the Kafka award, a Pushcart Prize, and the Howard Vursell Award of the American Academy of Arts and Letters.

Michael W. Lucas is an amateur aquariast, musique concrete aficionado, and a professional Internet backbone technician. He lives in an ancient flat in Grosse Pointe Park, Michigan, with assorted fish in the living room, several thousand books lining the walls, and a family of squirrels in the attic (the building's attic, not his). He's been engaged for four years. A graduate of Oakland University, his goal in life is to become either a professional writer or a llama smuggler, whichever seems more likely at the time.

Tom Piccirilli is the author of *Dark Father* and *Hexes and Shards.* He is assistant editor of *Pirate Writings* and *Space & Time* magazines, and reviews books for *Mystery News* and *The New York Review of Science Fiction.* His short fiction has appeared in *Hot Blood 6 & 7, 100 Wicked Little Witches, Deathrealm, The Silver Web,* as well as other magazines and anthologies. A collection of five intertwined tales entitled *Pentacle* was recently published by Pirate Writings Press, and his story "Eye-Biting and Other Displays of Affection" was nominated for the Bram Stoker Award for Best Novella.

About the Authors

Thomas S. Roche is a San Francisco writer whose stories have appeared in many horror and fantasy anthologies, including *Dark Angels, City of Darkness, Blood Muse, Enchanted Forests,* and in the erotic anthologies *Switch Hitters* and *Best Gay Erotica 1996,* among others. He has also made appearances in the magazines *Black Sheets, Paramour, Black Lotus,* and in Norway's *Cupido.*

Melanie Tem's most recent novels are *Witch-Light,* in collaboration with Nancy Holder (July 1996), and *Tides* (August 1996). Her short fiction has recently appeared in *Worlds of Fantasy and Horror, Peter Beagle's Immortal Unicorn, Dark Angels* and *High Fantastic.* She lives in Denver with her husband, writer and editor Steve Rasnic Tem. They have four children and two granddaughters.

About the Editor

Pam Keesey is a nice girl who wanted to grow up to be bad. She is the editor of *Daughters of Darkness* and *Dark Angels*, both collections of lesbian vampire stories. She is currently at work on *Vamps: An Illustrated Guide to Women as Vampires*, which explores vampire imagery from the ancient goddesses, the literary *femme fatales* of the nineteenth century and the vamps of the 1920s, to movie vampires and contemporary vamps such as Elvira and Sharon Stone.

BOOKS FROM CLEIS PRESS

SEXUAL POLITICS

Body Alchemy: Transsexual Portraits
by Loren Cameron.
ISBN: 1-57344-062-0 24.95 paper.

*Forbidden Passages: Writings
Banned in Canada*
introductions by Pat Califia
and Janine Fuller.
ISBN: 1-57344-019-1 14.95 paper.

*Good Sex: Real Stories
from Real People,*
second edition, by Julia Hutton.
ISBN: 1-57344-000-0 14.95 paper.

*The Good Vibrations Guide to Sex: How to
Have Safe, Fun Sex in the '90s* by Cathy
Winks and Anne Semans.
ISBN: 0-939416-84-0 16.95 paper.

*I Am My Own Woman: The Outlaw Life
of Charlotte von Mahlsdorf*
translated by Jean Hollander.
ISBN: 1-57344-010-8 12.95 paper.

*Madonnarama: Essays on Sex and
Popular Culture*
edited by Lisa Frank and Paul Smith.
ISBN: 0-939416-71-9 9.95 paper.

Public Sex: The Culture of Radical Sex
by Pat Califia.
ISBN: 0-939416-89-1 12.95 paper.

*Sex Work: Writings by Women in the Sex
Industry*
edited by Frédérique Delacoste
and Priscilla Alexander.
ISBN: 0-939416-11-5 16.95 paper.

*Susie Bright's Sexual Reality: A Virtual
Sex World Reader*
by Susie Bright.
ISBN: 0-939416-59-X 9.95 paper.

Susie Bright's Sexwise
by Susie Bright.
ISBN: 1-57344-002-7 10.95 paper.

Susie Sexpert's Lesbian Sex World
by Susie Bright.
ISBN: 0-939416-35-2 9.95 paper.

LESBIAN AND GAY STUDIES

Best Gay Erotica 1996
selected by Scott Heim,
edited by Michael Ford.
ISBN: 1-57344-052-3 12.95 paper.

Best Lesbian Erotica 1996
selected by Heather Lewis,
edited by Tristan Taormino.
ISBN: 1-57344-054-X 12.95 paper.

*The Case of the Good-For-Nothing
Girlfriend*
by Mabel Maney.
ISBN: 0-939416-91-3 10.95 paper.

The Case of the Not-So-Nice Nurse
by Mabel Maney.
ISBN: 0-939416-76-X 9.95 paper.

Dagger: On Butch Women
edited by Roxxie, Lily Burana,
Linnea Due.
ISBN: 0-939416-82-4 14.95 paper.

Dark Angels: Lesbian Vampire Stories
edited by Pam Keesey.
ISBN 1-7344-014-0 10.95 paper.

*Daughters of Darkness: Lesbian Vampire
Stories*
edited by Pam Keesey.
ISBN: 0-939416-78-6 9.95 paper.

*Different Daughters: A Book by Mothers
of Lesbians,* second edition,
edited by Louise Rafkin.
ISBN: 1-57344-050-7 12.95 paper.

*Different Mothers: Sons & Daughters of
Lesbians Talk About Their Lives*
edited by Louise Rafkin.
ISBN: 0-939416-41-7 9.95 paper.

*Dyke Strippers: Lesbian
Cartoonists A to Z*
edited by Roz Warren.
ISBN: 1-57344-008-6 16.95 paper.

*Girlfriend Number One: Lesbian Life in
the '90s*
edited by Robin Stevens.
ISBN: 0-939416-8 12.95 paper.

A Lesbian Love Advisor
by Celeste West.
ISBN: 0-939416-26-3 9.95 paper.

*More Serious Pleasure: Lesbian Erotic
Stories and Poetry*
edited by the Sheba Collective.
ISBN: 0-939416-47-6 9.95 paper.

**Nancy Clue and the Hardly Boys in *A
Ghost in the Closet***
by Mabel Maney.
ISBN: 1-57344-012-4 10.95 paper.

*The Night Audrey's Vibrator Spoke: A
Stonewall Riots Collection*
by Andrea Natalie.
ISBN: 0-939416-64-6 8.95 paper.

*Queer and Pleasant Danger:
Writing Out My Life*
by Louise Rafkin.
ISBN: 0-939416-61-1 9.95 paper.

*Revenge of Hothead Paisan: Homicidal
Lesbian Terrorist*
by Diane DiMassa.
ISBN: 1-57344-016-7 16.95 paper.

*Rubyfruit Mountain: A Stonewall Riots
Collection*
by Andrea Natalie.
ISBN: 0-939416-74-3 9.95 paper.

*Serious Pleasure: Lesbian Erotic Stories
and Poetry*
edited by the Sheba Collective.
ISBN: 0-939416-45-X 9.95 paper.

*Sons of Darkness: Tales of Men,
Blood and Immortality*
edited by Michael Rowe
and Thomas S. Roche.
ISBN: 1-57344-059-0 12.95 paper.

*Switch Hitters: Lesbians Write Gay Male
Erotica and Gay Men Write Lesbian Erotica*
edited by Carol Queen
and Lawrence Schimel.
ISBN: 1-57344-021-3 12.95 paper.

*Women Who Run with the Werewolves:
Tales of Blood, Lust and Metamorphosis*
edited by Pam Keesey.
ISBN: 1-57344-057-4 12.95 paper.

POLITICS OF HEALTH
*The Absence of the Dead Is Their
Way of Appearing*
by Mary Winfrey Trautmann.
ISBN: 0-939416-04-2 8.95 paper.

Don't: A Woman's Word
by Elly Danica.
ISBN: 0-939416-22-0 8.95 paper

*1 in 3: Women with Cancer Confront an
Epidemic*
edited by Judith Brady.
ISBN: 0-939416-49-2 10.95 paper.

*Voices in the Night: Women Speaking
About Incest*
edited by Toni A.H. McNaron
and Yarrow Morgan.
ISBN: 0-939416-02-6 9.95 paper.

*With the Power of Each Breath: A
Disabled Women's Anthology*
edited by Susan Browne,
Debra Connors and Nanci Stern.
ISBN: 0-939416-06-9 10.95 paper.

REFERENCE
*Betty and Pansy's Severe Queer Review of
San Francisco*
by Betty Pearl and Pansy.
ISBN: 1-57344-056-6 10.95 paper.

Food for Life & Other Dish,
edited by Lawrence Schimel.
ISBN: 1-57344-061-2 14.95 paper.

Putting Out: The Essential Publishing
Resource Guide For Gay and Lesbian
Writers, third edition,
by Edisol W. Dotson.
ISBN: 0-939416-87-5 12.95 paper.

FICTION
Cosmopolis: Urban Stories by Women
edited by Ines Rieder.
ISBN: 0-939416-37-9 9.95 paper.

Dirty Weekend: A Novel of Revenge
by Helen Zahavi.
ISBN: 0-939416-85-9 10.95 paper.

A Forbidden Passion
by Cristina Peri Rossi.
ISBN: 0-939416-68-9 9.95 paper.

Half a Revolution: Contemporary Fiction
by Russian Women
edited by Masha Gessen.
ISBN 1-57344-006-X $12.95 paper.

In the Garden of Dead Cars
by Sybil Claiborne.
ISBN: 0-939416-66-2 9.95 paper.

Memory Mambo
by Achy Obejas.
ISBN: 1-57344-017-5 12.95 paper.

Night Train To Mother
by Ronit Lentin.
ISBN: 0-939416-28-X 9.95 paper.

Only Lawyers Dancing
by Jan McKemmish.
ISBN: 0-939416-69-7 9.95 paper.

Seeing Dell
by Carol Guess
ISBN: 1-57344-023-X 12.95 paper.

The Wall
by Marlen Haushofer.
ISBN: 0-939416-54-9 paper.

We Came All The Way from Cuba So
You Could Dress Like This?: Stories
by Achy Obejas.
ISBN: 0-939416-93-X 10.95 paper.

LATIN AMERICA
The Little School: Tales of Disappearance
and Survival in Argentina
by Alicia Partnoy.
ISBN: 0-939416-07-7 9.95 paper.

Revenge of the Apple
by Alicia Partnoy.
ISBN: 0-939416-63-8 8.95 paper.

AUTOBIOGRAPHY, BIOGRAPHY,
LETTERS
Peggy Deery: An Irish Family at War
by Nell McCafferty.
ISBN: 0-939416-39-5 9.95 paper.

The Shape of Red: Insider/Outsider
Reflections
by Ruth Hubbard and Margaret Randall.
ISBN: 0-939416-18-2 9.95 paper.

Women & Honor:
Some Notes on Lying
by Adrienne Rich.
ISBN: 0-939416-44-1 3.95 paper.

Ordering Information

Since 1980, Cleis Press has published progressive books by women. We welcome your order and will ship your books as quickly as possible. Individual orders must be prepaid (U.S. dollars only). Please add 15% shipping. PA residents add 6% sales tax. Mail orders to:

Cleis Press
PO Box 8933
Pittsburgh PA 15221.

MasterCard and Visa orders: include account number, exp. date, and signature. FAX your credit card order: (412) 937-1567. Or, phone us Mon-Fri, 9 am - 5 pm EST: (412) 937-1555 or (800) 780-2279.